'What is it? What's wrong?' he asked her, coming over to her. She had to sit down. She couldn't stand up a second longer, she felt so weak, so terrified of what was happening to her.

Ben dropped on his knees beside her, so close to her that his robe gaped slightly as he moved.

'What is it? What's wrong?' he demanded again.

She couldn't stand it a moment longer. Everything that she was suffering welled up inside her, and before she could stop herself she burst out frantically, 'It's you. It's... Oh, for heaven's sake, can't you put some clothes on...?'

*Books you will enjoy*
*by PENNY JORDAN*

### SECOND TIME LOVING

Daniel Forbes was attractive, charming and made it clear he would welcome Angelica into his bed. Having been used by gold-digger Giles, Angelica had vowed not to let any other man make a fool of her, but, try as she might, she found Daniel impossible to resist . . .

### PAYMENT DUE

Tania couldn't find a way to convince James Warren that she was an innocent bystander to the tangle of lies and deceit that surrounded his stepsister's marriage. James was a threat to her new life with her daughter, which was a pity, because in other circumstances she could have found him very attractive . . .

### A FORBIDDEN LOVING

Silas Jardine was Katie's boyfriend. And he was only being nice to Hazel because she was Katie's mother. The fact that Silas was more than twenty years older than Katie was something that Hazel would just have to come to terms with—as was the fact that she found him devastatingly attractive . . .

### A TIME TO DREAM

Melanie was delighted when a total stranger left her all his worldly goods, including a country cottage. But she discovered that her windfall brought its own problems. Take her attractive neighbour, Luke Chalmers—was his more than friendly interest genuine, or did he have something to hide?

# DANGEROUS INTERLOPER

BY

PENNY JORDAN

MILLS & BOON LIMITED
ETON HOUSE    18-24 PARADISE ROAD
RICHMOND    SURREY    TW9 1SR

First published in Great Britain 1991
by Mills & Boon Limited

© Penny Jordan 1991

Australian copyright 1991
Philippine copyright 1991
This edition 1991

ISBN 0 263 77230 6

Set in Times Roman 11 on 12 pt.
01-9109-47542 C

Made and printed in Great Britain

# CHAPTER ONE

MIRANDA SHEPHERD paused on the pavement, staring up through the scaffolding at the building in front of her. Her heart sank. So it had started, then. What had once been an admittedly shabby but untouched Georgian town house had now fallen victim to the developers' greedy and uncaring hands.

It had been happening so often lately, especially since their quiet country town had become so easily accessible to London.

Whereas once shoppers had clustered happily and untidily around the small market square and its surrounding warren of narrow cobbled streets, they were now abandoning these old-fashioned local shops for the new hypermarket and enclosed shopping centre which had recently been constructed on the edge of the town, leaving its once thriving centre empty.

As the leases had fallen due for renewal they had been bought up, and slowly, one by one, the shabby Georgian town houses were being redeveloped and sold off to the new breed of businesses taking over the centre of the town; building societies, banks, estate agencies like her father's, and offices.

This building had been a particular favourite of Miranda's and to see it fall into the hands of what she privately considered to be one of the town's least sympathetic and most greedy builders had saddened and outraged her. She wasn't alone in her resentment and anger either, even though her father might gently point out that people had to make a living and that the rash of newcomers and new businesses to the area was also bringing with it new jobs. A conservation group had sprung up to protect what was left of the town's heritage, although in the case of this particular house it was already too late.

The building had, she learned from her father, been sold to another newcomer; a businessman from London who wanted to base his computer-software business in the town.

She shuddered inwardly, able to imagine all too easily how the house would look when it was finished, stripped of its faded elegance and 'improved' to meet the demands of its new owner.

As she was staring sadly at the yawning windows, now minus their elegant sash frames, she was hailed by a man coming out of the front door.

'Well, if it isn't Miranda, and looking as stunning as ever... Looking for me, were you, my lovely? I'm just about to knock off. Fancy coming and having a bite of lunch with me?' Miranda froze, cursing her own folly in stopping. She might have known that, with her luck, Ralph Charlesworth would be here. It was his building firm which was doing the renovations, and that on its own would have been sufficient to ensure that she was not well-disposed towards him; but added to that was the fact that he was a swaggering, unpleasantly arrogant man, who at thirty-five with a wife and three small children still seemed to think he was free to behave as though they simply did not exist.

For some reason he was at present insisting on pursuing Miranda, although she had made it more than plain to him that she was not only not interested, but she found his heavy-handed flirtatiousness offensive and unwelcome. Even if he had not been married, she would not have found him attractive, either physically or mentally.

He was a big man, rather overweight, with small, rather unpleasantly close-set eyes and a manner of looking at her that made her skin crawl.

Now, as she inwardly cursed the misfortune which had made her stop to look at the house just as he happened to be emerging from it, she told him coldly, 'No, as a matter of fact I *wasn't* looking for you.'

'No?'

The disbelieving leer he gave her made her face flush with renewed anger.

In her view it was unfortunate that, through her job as a very junior partner in her father's estate agency business, she was obliged in certain circumstances to come into contact with Ralph.

On these occasions she was always icily and coldly formal with him, making sure she never gave him any reason to believe she was anything other than repulsed by his apparent interest in her.

Her father had sympathetically offered to make sure she came into as little contact with the builder as possible, but she had shaken her head determinedly. After all, she couldn't hide behind her father's protection all her life. Ralph Charlesworth

and men like him were just one of the more unpleasant aspects of her chosen career.

She was a tall woman, but very slenderly built,
with fragile-looking bones, and a delicately heart-
shaped face framed by a soft straight bob of silky
black hair.

In her own view her eyes were her best feature,
being almond shaped and wide apart, and a colour
which varied from blue to lavender, depending on
her mood.

Right now they were the colour of the storm
clouds which lined the horizon on blustery days,
tinged almost purple with the weight of her anger
and dislike.

Up above her on the scaffolding she could hear
some of Ralph's men calling out jocular comments
to him. No doubt his men didn't mean to be
personally offensive to her, she reflected bitterly as
she turned away from the building; no doubt,
working as they did for a man like Ralph, they took
their cue from him and perhaps thought it flattering to call out personal and often offensively
personal remarks to any woman foolish or unwary
enough to walk past them. She personally found
such behaviour unwarranted and unpleasant.

'Aw, come on ... With a figure like yours, you
can't need to worry about calories,' Ralph leered,
openly letting his gaze slide lasciviously over her
body.

To her humiliation, Miranda felt her face flushing
as guiltily as though she had in some way invited
the intrusiveness of his sexual appraisal of her.

Surely her neat pleated skirt, with its complementary tailored jacket over a crisp white blouse, could never be even remotely described as provocative, and as for her manner...she was sure that at no time had she ever given Ralph Charlesworth the slightest reason to believe that she even liked him, never mind...

All too conscious of the attention she was drawing from the watching men above her, Miranda decided there was no point in allowing herself to be drawn into any further change of conversation, so she turned on her heel and walked angrily away, her mind seething with anger and resentment as she turned the corner and headed for the town square.

As she rounded the corner the wind caught her hair, whipping it across her eyes, momentarily blinding her so that she didn't see the man coming towards her until it was too late and she had walked right into him.

'Hey, are you all right?'

'All right...' The words reverberated dizzily somewhere deep within her, causing the most odd sensations inside her. Or was it the firm pressure of those male arms, the proximity of that hard male chest which rose and fell so...so steadily and somehow comfortingly against her own that was causing her to experience this odd light-headedness?

Shakily she fought to control her peculiar responses, pushing herself away from the warmth of his body, and drawing herself up to her full height as she forced herself to at least try to look businesslike and cool.

'Yes…yes…I'm fine…so silly of me…I wasn't looking where I was going.'

She looked at him as she spoke and suffered such a shock of sensation through her entire body that it was as though she had suddenly become completely paralysed.

She was a tall girl, but this man … was taller—six feet two at least. He had broad shoulders, very broad shoulders, she acknowledged weakly as she discovered she was still staring at him.

'Oh, is that what it was?' His voice was warm and deep, and laced with something that suggested that he had a good sense of humour. 'I rather had the impression you were trying to escape from something or someone.'

She couldn't help it; Miranda knew that her eyes were widening automatically in reaction to his perceptiveness. Instinctively she looked up into his eyes, and then immediately wished she hadn't. They were warm and grey, and fringed with thick dark lashes. She couldn't remember the last time a man, any man, had had such an intense physical impact on her. Come on, she warned herself, you're twenty-eight, not eighteen. You do not walk into a stranger and then stand staring at him as dumbstruck as though you've fallen head over heels in love with him, even if he does come packaged six feet-odd, grey eyed, dark-haired and with the most devastating smile you've ever seen.

It's the inner person who matters, not his outward physical appearance, she told herself severely as she tried to pull herself together, and realised that he was still smiling at her as though waiting for a response to his comment.

The very idea of explaining to him about Ralph Charlesworth was far too impossible even to be contemplated and so instead she launched into a breathless rush of semi-truths, explaining to him that it was the sight of the desecration of what had once been a wonderful example of small-town Georgian architecture that had sent her scurrying round the corner without paying attention to what she was doing.

'Still, I suppose this computer genius who's bought the place doesn't know how important it is to preserve buildings like this one; nor if he did, would he care.'

As she came to a breathless full stop, his eyebrows arched. 'That's a rather biased criticism, isn't it?' he suggested mildly.

Miranda felt her face flush uncomfortably, aware that she had probably sounded more overheated than their very brief acquaintance warranted.

She also realised several other things as well: namely that she was deliberately if unconsciously delaying taking her leave of him; that she could have quite easily stood for hours here on the pavement looking at him; that she was going to be late arriving back at the office; that she was in fact behaving like a complete fool, and should have simply thanked him and apologised to him for bumping into him in a crisp businesslike manner and gone on her way.

'I . . . I must go,' she told him quickly. 'I'm sorry I delayed you . . .'

She hesitated, half hoping he would make some kind of gallant comment about it being a pleasure to be delayed by her, and half relieved when he didn't. If there was one thing that ordinarily she detested, it was heavy-handed compliments, and yet to know that this particular man had found her company pleasurable...

Angry with herself, she stepped hurriedly past him, walking quickly into the square and then across it.

Their office was on the other side of the square in a pretty Queen Anne town house, which her father had bought when he'd originally set up his practice in the town.

She didn't allow herself to look back, but that didn't stop her thoughts from wondering busily who he was. Ruefully she told herself that he was very probably married with a family, chiding herself for her interest in him. She hadn't seen him around before, but that didn't mean anything. The town was growing, mushrooming almost, and whereas when she'd first joined her father in his estate agency business as his junior partner she could hardly walk across the town square without stopping to acknowledge the greetings of almost everyone she passed, now the opposite was true.

Liz, their receptionist, gave her a sunny smile when she walked in.

'Dad's in his office, is he?' she asked her.

'Yes. He's going out in half an hour, though, to show some clients round Frenshaw's farm.'

Thanking her, Miranda walked through the pleasant, comfortable reception area and into the passage beyond it. Three doors led off the passage, one to her father's office, one to her own, and one that they used as a general filing and storage space.

As she rapped briefly on her father's office door before walking in, she found herself thinking about the man again, wondering who he was and where he had been going.

Stop it, she told herself severely. She was a woman of twenty-eight, who had firmly and deliberately avoided what she considered to be the pitfalls of falling in love and committing herself to the kind of marriage she had seen overwhelm so many of her friends.

Maybe in the large cities things were different, but here in this country town—and, she suspected, in others like it—a woman was still expected to be the mainstay of the family in the traditional way.

Oh, perhaps these days a woman had a job as well, but, from what Miranda could see of her friends' lives, this made things harder for them and not easier. It might give them some financial independence, but in return for that they had to suffer losing the independence of having time to themselves, and to shoulder an extra burden of guilt, especially when they had children.

Most of her friends had married in their early twenties, when the last thing she had wanted had been the constraints of having to put another person's desires and needs before her own. She liked being free to make her own decisions about how she should spend her life and her time. She knew that in the eyes of many of her friends she was well and truly established as a bachelor girl and a career woman, and originally this hadn't bothered her, but lately she had begun to undergo some kind of sea change; a totally unexpected sea change, it had to be admitted.

For the first time, she had recently picked up a friend's new baby, expecting to experience her normal lack of interest but ready to make all the appropriate noises to satisfy the new mother's pride, and had instead experienced the most peculiar sense of completeness, of wanting to go on holding the small warm body; so much so that when she had handed the baby back to its mother she had actually felt a tiny ache of loss.

She had quickly put the experience behind her, telling herself that it was simply a momentary aberration; something hormonal that was unlikely to happen again. Only she had been wrong.

She hoped she was far too sensible to mistake this unfamiliar yearning for a mate and his offspring for anything other than a probable reaction to too much not-so-subtle pressure from the media to conform to the image of the modern woman, who, according to them, in order to be fulfilled must 'have it all'. Certainly she had already ruefully decided that the chances of her finding a man with whom she might want to actually spend the rest of her life locally were very small indeed.

She had a large circle of friends, enjoyed their company, both male and female, but none of the men she knew had ever aroused anything more than a mild degree of friendship within her. At least until today...

'Ah, there you are,' her father greeted her as she walked into his office. 'You haven't forgotten about tonight, have you?'

'Tonight?'

'Yes, the dinner dance at the golf club. I told you about it,' he reminded her. 'I've invited Ben Frobisher, the man who bought the house in the High Street.'

'The computer man?' Miranda asked grimly. 'Oh, you *know* how I feel about what's happening to the town . . . to its buildings. I walked past there this morning. Ralph Charlesworth's got the contract for the work.' Her face hardened a little. 'That building ought to have been listed. We've been in touch with the Georgian Society and they confirmed——'

'Look, Miranda, I know how you feel,' her father interrupted her patiently, 'but this man's an important client. He'll have employees who will be wanting to relocate in the area. He himself is looking for a house. He's renting the Elshaw place at the moment.'

'If he's as high-profile as you say, I can't understand why he should want to attend the annual golf club hop,' Miranda told her father drily.

'I expect he wants to get to know people. After all, he is going to be a part of the community.'

'Is he? From what I've seen, most of the people who've moved down here seem to prefer to form their own small smart cliques rather than try to integrate with the locals. Look at what's happened at the tennis club.

'This time last year we had four tatty courts that were only used in the summer and a club-house that was falling down; now, thanks to a small high-pressure group of London wives, we've got a building fund going and ambitious plans to build two indoor courts, plus all the facilities of an expensive London gym, complete with swimming pool, bar, and everything that goes with it.'

'So? What's wrong with that?'

'Dad, don't you see? It's spoiling the character of the place. Another few years and we'll just be another dormitory town. The locals won't be able to afford to live here any more, and during the week it will be a town of too rich, too bored women vying with one another.

'There won't be any real life to the town; it will be completely sanitised. There'll be no children—they'll all be away at boarding school. There won't be any old people—they'll all be packed off to exclusive residential homes.'

'If that means that we'll no longer have a dozen or more surly-looking youths hanging round the town square all night, then personally I think it would be a good thing.'

'But, Dad, those kids belong here, and they're not surly. They're just...just young,' Miranda told him helplessly. One of her extramural activities which gave her the most satisfaction was her work with a local youth club. 'They need an outlet for their energy, that's all,' she told her father. 'And they won't find it in some expensive exclusive tennis club.'

He laughed, shook his head and smiled ruefully at her.

'I think you're over-reacting a little, Miranda. Don't forget that people like Ben Frobisher are bringing new life to the area, new jobs...new opportunities.'

'New architecture,' Miranda murmured under her breath, unable to resist.

Her father looked at her. 'You don't *know* what he intends to do with that house. He struck me as an eminently sensible man. I'm sure that he——'

'Sensible? And yet he still employed Ralph Charlesworth?'

Her father sighed. 'All right. I know you don't like Ralph Charlesworth; admittedly he isn't the most prepossessing of men, but he does have a good reputation as a builder. He's tough and he sticks to his contracts.'

Miranda shook her head, knowing that this was a subject on which she and her father would never agree. That was what made her job so enjoyable, though: the fact that they were so different...had views which were sometimes so conflicting. Her father admitted that since she had joined the firm their business had improved dramatically, and equally she was the first to concede that without her father's experience, his 'know-how', his tolerance, she would never have been able to branch out into testing ideas which were innovative and new.

They made a good team, she recognised as she smiled at him.

'Don't forget,' he warned her, 'about tonight; I've arranged for Frobisher to meet us at home, and we'll all set off from there. It will make things easier.'

'What time do you want me there?' Miranda asked him, giving in. She didn't live with her father, but had her own small cottage several miles outside the town.

'Half-past seven,' he told her. 'Helen is arriving at seven.'

Helen Johnson was a widow some five years younger than her father. They had become engaged at Christmas...and were getting married at the end of the month. They were then going on a month's cruise, leaving Miranda in sole charge of the business.

She liked Helen and was pleased that her father was remarrying. Her mother had always had a weak heart, and after a long period of illness had died several days after Miranda's twelfth birthday.

Miranda had missed her desperately; had gone through anguish, anger, fear and despair, had hated both her mother for leaving her and her father for letting her, but eventually she had begun to recover, and by the time she was in her late teens had become mature enough to understand that if she missed her mother so desperately then her father must feel even more alone.

She had been twenty-one when her father had offered her her partnership in the business, and it was then that she had decided to find her own home, as much for her father's sake as her own. He was an attractive man, still only in his mid-

fifties, and, although he never seemed to be interested in any of the women who pursued him,
Miranda had felt that it was only fair to him not
to burden him with a live-in grown-up daughter.

He had met Helen three years ago, when she had
come into their offices to ask their advice on selling
her large house following the death of her husband.
What she wanted was to stay in the area, but in
something rather smaller, she had told them.

It had originally been Miranda who had dealt
with her, and who had convinced her to buy a very
pretty Georgian house on the outskirts of the town,
convenient for everything, and yet still quiet, with
a pleasant garden and pretty views over the river
and the surrounding countryside.

Now she and Miranda's father were getting
married and Miranda was delighted for both of
them.

What did not delight her quite so much was the
fact that Ralph Charlesworth's wife was Helen's
niece.

Not that she had anything against Susan
Charlesworth. In fact she considered her a very
pleasant, if somewhat introverted woman. What
she did not like was the fact that as Helen's niece
she would be attending the wedding. Which meant
that her husband would also be attending the
wedding . . . which meant that she, Miranda, would
be forced to endure his company for a number of
hours and to be pleasant to him in the interests of
family harmony, and yet at the same time reinforce
to him her complete rejection of him as a man.

She had no idea why he had decided to make her the object of his pursuit. She had certainly given him no encouragement to do so. She found him detestable and felt thoroughly sorry for Susan Charlesworth. The next time she found herself going all maternal and gooey-eyed over someone's baby, she might try reminding herself of how much she would loathe being married to a man like Ralph Charlesworth, she told herself wryly as she settled down to work.

She worked steadily all afternoon, reflecting that the influx of people into the area had certainly brought a dramatic increase in the firm's business, and that if things kept on the way they were going her father would have to consider taking on another partner.

At half-past five her father himself rapped on her office door and opened it.

'Don't forget about tonight, will you?' he asked her.

'No. I promise I'll be there.'

Just as he was about to leave she asked, 'Doesn't this Ben Frobisher have a wife? He's in his thirties, isn't he?'

'Thirty-four, and no, he doesn't have a wife. He's never been married and seems to be quite content with his single state. A bit like you,' he pointed out slyly, grinning at her when she glowered threateningly at him.

After he'd gone, she tried to concentrate on her work, but for some reason her thoughts kept sliding back to the man she had bumped into earlier and at last, in exasperation, she put down her pen and leaned her chin on her hand, frowning into space.

It was ridiculous to keep thinking about him like this. A stranger... a total stranger, who, for all the thoughtful interest she could have sworn she had seen glinting in his eyes, had made no attempt to make any capital out of the situation fate had thrown them into and suggest extending their acquaintance.

Not that she would have wanted him to come on to her in the manner of the likes of the Ralph Charlesworths of this world, she told herself hastily, but a subtle compliment and the suggestion that he would not have been averse to seeing her again...

For heaven's sake, she derided herself, trying to dismiss him from her mind. She was a woman, not a teenager, and it wasn't even as though she didn't have a hundred better things to occupy her thoughts.

Tomorrow night, for instance, there was a meeting of the newly formed Committee for the Preservation of Local Buildings. She had been asked if she would like to be its president, but she had hastily declined, explaining that her other responsibilities meant that, although she would be an enthusiastic supporter of their work, she could not take charge of it and do it justice.

The others on the committee were all locals; Tim Ford, a local historian and schoolteacher, now retired; the vicar's wife; Linda Smithson, the doctor's wife; and a couple of others. Miranda was also due to attend another meeting the following night, to decide how best they could organise something within the town which would prove of sufficient interest to its youth to keep them from loitering boredly in the town square.

Yes, she had more than enough to occupy her time and her thoughts without allowing them to drift helplessly and dangerously in the direction of a man she didn't really know and whom she was hardly likely to see again.

The trouble was, though...the trouble was that nature had seen fit to bestow her with a rather over-active imagination. Something which on occasions she found to be rather a trial, especially when she was trying to concentrate on promoting a cool and businesslike professional image.

Right now it was rebelliously insisting on coaxing her away from her work, and into an extremely unlikely but very alluring daydream in which, instead of releasing her so promptly and so courteously as he had done, the stranger had held on to her that little bit longer, had gazed deeply and meaningfully into her eyes until her whole body tingled with the sensual message of that look.

Almost without knowing she was doing it, she had closed her eyes and relaxed in her chair.

Of course, she would have tried to pull away, to convey with the cool remoteness of her withdrawal that she was not in the least impressed or flattered by his interest. And of course she would be able to look directly and unmovingly at the sensual curve of that very male mouth without feeling the slightest tremor inside her, even while she was aware that he was still holding on to her and that his gaze was fastened on her mouth in a way that in her day-dream made her give a tiny sigh.

Of course he wouldn't kiss her in broad daylight in the middle of the street. Of course he wouldn't, couldn't, but he could release her slowly and regretfully, so that his fingers held on to her arms as though he couldn't bring himself to break his physical contact with her, and of course before he let her go he had made sure that he knew both her name and where he could get in touch with her.

'Miranda. Oh, I'm sorry, I didn't mean to wake you.'

Miranda jolted upright in her chair, opening her eyes as Liz came in.

'I . . . I—er—wasn't asleep,' she told her guiltily. 'I . . . I've . . . got a bit of headache.'

'Oh, dear, and you're going out to that golf club do tonight, aren't you?' Liz sympathised. 'I hope it goes before then.'

Tell one lie and you had to tell a round dozen to back it up, Miranda reflected to herself half an hour later as she drove homewards. And what on earth had possessed her anyway? Allowing her mind to drift in that idiotic silly fashion. Good heavens, she had thought she was well past the stage of such idiocy. Daydreams of that kind belonged to one's very early teens alongside fruitless dreams over thankfully out-of-reach pop stars.

She put her foot down a little harder on her accelerator. Well, tonight should bring her down to earth with a bump. She only hoped that Ben Frobisher didn't prove to be too boring. No doubt he would talk about computers all night long, which meant she would hardly be able to understand a thing he was saying.

Her cottage was small and rather isolated, its timber frame sunk into the ground as though crumpling under the burden of its heavy stone roof.

When she had originally bought the cottage it had been little more than a shell. It had taken a good deal of work and research to transform it into the home it was now.

The setting sun harmonised with the soft colour of its peachy-pink-washed exterior walls. She had made the lime wash herself, and dyed it, using a traditional recipe and ingredients. That result had only been achieved after several attempts, but it had been well worth the effort she had put in.

Inside she had taken just as much care over the renovation of her small rooms and the purchase of the furniture which clothed them.

The back door opened straight into a square stone-flagged kitchen. The cat curled up on top of the Aga greeted her with a soft purr of pleasure.

'You don't fool me. I know it's only cupboard-love, William,' she told him as she scratched behind his ears.

There was no point in making a meal, not when she would be eating out later. A quick snack, a cup of coffee and then she would have to go upstairs and get ready to go out.

She made a wry face to herself. There were a dozen things she'd rather be doing tonight than playing the dutiful daughter and partner, but she had promised her father.

# CHAPTER TWO

WELL her dress was hardly designer style, Miranda reflected, studying her image critically in her mirror, but then the golf club was not exactly the haunt of the beautiful people. Most of the members were around her father's age, pleasant enough but inclined to be a little dull. She wondered cynically if their new client realised what he was letting himself in for, and then told herself that she was perhaps being a little unfair.

Biased...that was what *he* had called her. She stopped looking at herself, her eyes becoming soft and dreamy. Now, if she had been going out with him tonight, she wouldn't have been satisfied with her simple plain black dress and her mother's pearls, she reflected, not seeing as others did, that the slender elegance of her body somehow made the simple understatement of her plain dress all the more appealing and eye-catching in a way that would never have occurred to her. If anyone had told her that the silky swing of her hair, the soft sheen of her skin and the plain simplicity of her clothes all added up to a sensuality all the more effective because it was so obviously unstudied, she wouldn't have believed them, but it was true none the less.

Tartly reminding herself that, since the object of her ridiculous daydreams had not appeared the least

25

bit interested in her, it was pointless wasting her time fretting about the clothes she didn't have to wear if he asked her out, she clipped on her pearl earrings and picked up her bag.

All through her schooldays her teachers had bemoaned her tendency to daydream. She had thought in the last few years that she had finally outgrown it. Now it seemed she had been over-optimistic.

It took her just over half an hour to drive to her father's house on the other side of town. Helen's car was already parked in the drive, and when Miranda went up to the front door it was Helen who opened it to her.

At her father's insistence she still had a key for her old home, but she only used it when he was away on holiday, just to check that the house and its contents were safe.

Helen kissed her and greeted her warmly. She wasn't as tall as Miranda, a still-pretty fair-haired woman of fifty, whom Miranda doubted anyone could ever have disliked. She had a natural warmth, a genuine compassion for humanity that Miranda could only describe as a very special kind of motherliness, and that made her wish sometimes that her father had met her earlier and that she could have had the benefit of her compassion and love during her own difficult teenage years, although she was honest enough to admit that, had her father met her then, she would probably not have responded well to her and would have been inclined to be jealous and possessive of her father.

'Dad not ready yet?' Miranda queried as she closed the door behind her.

'You know your father,' Helen said humorously. 'He says he can't find his cufflinks.'

Miranda laughed. 'It's just as well you're organising everything for the wedding. How's it going by the way? Have you found *the* outfit yet?'

Helen had complained to her only the week before that she had still not found an outfit she liked enough to wear for the supposedly quiet church wedding organised for the end of the month.

'No, I haven't. I've decided that I'm going to have to have a day in Bath or maybe even in London.' Helen pulled a face. 'I'm dreading it. I loathe city shopping.'

They chatted easily together for a few minutes while they waited for Miranda's father to come downstairs.

Just as he did so, they heard a car coming up the drive.

'This will be Ben Frobisher!' her father exclaimed, hurrying towards the door and opening it.

As she heard the sound of male footsteps crunching over the gravel, Miranda slipped discreetly into the shadows at the rear of the hall so that she would have a good view of her partner for the evening, without his being similarly able to observe her.

She watched as he mounted the steps and came forward into the light, and then her heart turned over with shock, and she stared with open disbelief, closing her eyes and then opening them again; but no, she wasn't daydreaming; it was the stranger, the man she had bumped into earlier on. He was standing there, calmly returning her father's hand-

shake, turning to smile warmly at Helen, his dark
hair shining cleanly and healthily beneath the light,
his tall broad-shouldered body moving easily within
the elegant confines of his dinner suit, his eyes as
familiarly and perceptively grey as she had remembered as they swept the shadows.

'Miranda, come and meet Ben,' her father called
out to her, forcing her to move forward, to extend
her hand and to force her lips into what she hoped
was a sophisticated and cool smile.

'Actually Mr Frobisher and I have already met.'
His handshake was firm, if brief.

'Ben, please,' he corrected her.

'You two know each other?' Miranda heard her
father saying curiously. 'But, Miranda, you
never——'

'We met by chance earlier on today. At the time
your daughter was escaping from the depressing
sight of my desecration of what she informed me
had once been a fine old Georgian building.' His
eyebrows lifted humorously as he smiled at
Miranda. 'She was a little—er—angry, and I didn't
think it wise to introduce myself.'

'Oh, Miranda is one of the leading lights of our
newly formed Committee for the Preservation of
Local Buildings,' Miranda heard her father saying
while to her own fury she could feel her face
flushing.

'It isn't quite as bad as you seem to think, you
know,' Ben Frobisher told her, still smiling at her,
adding, 'In fact, why don't you give me an opportunity to prove it to you? Let me show you the plans
I've had drawn up.'

'By Ralph Charlesworth?' Miranda demanded scornfully, letting her temper and her embarrassment get the better of her.

The whole evening was going to be a complete disaster. She could tell that already... Of all the humiliating things to have happened... had he known who she was when...? But no, he couldn't have.

'No, not by Charlesworth, as it happens.'

That made her focus on him and then immediately wish she had not done so, as she was subjected to the fully dizzying effect of meeting that level grey gaze head on.

It was like running full tilt into an immovable object, she reflected, the effect just as instant and even more of a shock to the system. Her heart was beating too fast; she was fighting not to breathe too quickly and shallowly. She felt slightly dizzy and thoroughly bemused. It was totally unfair that he should affect her like this.

'I'm sure Miranda would be delighted to see them,' she could hear her father saying heartily at her side. 'Wouldn't you, Mirry?'

Wouldn't she what? she wondered muzzily, somehow or other managing to force herself to respond with a brief inclination of her head and a rather wobbly smile.

'I'm delighted that you were able to join us tonight, Ben!' Miranda heard her father exclaiming. 'They're a good crowd at the club.'

Behind her father's back, Miranda grimaced slightly to herself and then flushed wildly as something made her look up and she saw that Ben Frobisher was watching her.

'And you, Miranda,' he enquired politely, 'do you play golf?'

Her father answered for her, chuckling.

'Not Mirry. She doesn't have the patience. She plays tennis, though...'

'Tennis. It's becoming very fashionable at the moment.'

For some reason the musing comment delivered in Ben Frobisher's very male voice made her stiffen and look defensively at him. She had the feeling that his comment had been slightly barbed...slightly derogatory.

'I've been playing ever since I left school,' she told him challengingly, adding pointedly just in case he hadn't got the message, 'long before it became fashionable.'

As they walked out to the car, Miranda tried to quell her mixed feelings of irritation and embarrassment and then reflected how very different reality was from her daydreams. In them she had perceived Ben Frobisher as a highly desirable stranger, who also desired her; in reality... In reality he quite plainly did nothing of the kind, and there was an abrasion between them, a covert hostility that was making her feel both uncomfortable and defensive.

It was all because she had made that stupid unguarded comment about the house, of course. And the only reason she had said that had been that she didn't want to admit to him that he had been right and that she *had* been escaping from something and someone, namely Ralph Charlesworth and his pursuit of her. Well, it was too late now to wish she had not acted so impulsively. Much too late. But how could she have guessed who he was? She had imagined that the then unknown Ben Frobisher would be a much smaller man, hunch-shouldered and probably bespectacled, as befitted someone who spent long hours staring at a computer screen working out complex programs.

This man looked as though he had spent more time outdoors than in, although she ought to have been warned by the unmistakable intelligence and shrewdness in those grey eyes.

'I thought we'd all travel together in my car,' her father suggested, and before she could argue and insist on taking her own car Miranda discovered that Ben Frobisher was politely holding open one of the rear doors of her father's BMW for her and that she had no option but to get in. When he went round the other side of the car and got in beside her, she could literally feel her muscles tensing.

Not against *him*, she recognised miserably, but against *herself*, against her own involuntary reaction to him.

Hell, she swore crossly to herself. This was the last thing she needed...an inconvenient and definitely unwanted sexual reaction to a man whom she had now made up her mind she did not like.

All right, so maybe it *wasn't* his fault that she had made such a fool of herself, but somehow, illogically, her emotions refused to accept this. There had been no reason for him to mention what she had said about the house in front of her father and

Helen, had there? It was bad enough that *he* knew how tactless she had been, and as for looking at his precious plans... She tensed again as she realised belatedly that she had already accepted his offer. That would teach her to let her mind wander and not to concentrate on what was going on around her! With good reason had her teachers rebuked her for daydreaming.

Teachers? She wasn't a schoolgirl now, she was a woman...an independent career woman. An independent career woman who wilfully daydreamed about unknown men? She chewed unhappily on her bottom lip, angry with herself as well as with the man sitting silently beside her.

The evening was going to be a total and utter disaster, she knew it.

As her father drove them towards the golf club, she told herself that it served her right and that this was what came of allowing herself to weave idiotic daydreams around a man she didn't really know.

Had she known who he was when they met... She frowned to herself as she stared out into the darkness of the surrounding landscape.

Would his physical impact on her have been lessened if she *had* known who he was? She wasn't a young girl any more, after all; a person's personality, their beliefs, their sense of humour, their views of life and love—it was important that all these should mesh with and complement her own, and anyone who could employ someone like Ralph Charlesworth to undertake the renovation of a graceful old house like the one Ben Frobisher had bought could not possibly have the same outlook on life as herself. Which was probably just as well. After all, he had not shown any reciprocal awareness of her interest in her—quite the reverse— so the sensible, indeed, the *essential* thing for her to do was to forget the disruptive physical effect that that first unexpected meeting had had on her and to concentrate instead on the reality of the man he was actually proving to be.

A very sensible and mature decision to come to; so why, at the same time as she was congratulating herself on this sensible mature outlook, was she also angrily wishing that she had dressed with a little more *élan*, a little more sophistication; that she had perhaps made the effort to take herself off to Bath and buy herself a new dress?

A new dress for the golf club dance—and when she had promised herself that this year she intended to save up and treat herself to a holiday in Hong Kong and the Far East? What on earth was happening to her?

Nothing, she told herself firmly, answering her own question; nothing whatsoever was happening to her, and nothing was *going* to happen to her.

Even so, when the lights of the club-house came into view she found herself wishing that the evening was already over and that she was safely tucked up in her cosy cottage bedroom.

Something about Ben Frobisher made her feel acutely unsure of herself; acutely aware of him as a man, and of her own reactions to that maleness.

She moved uncomfortably in her seat. She didn't like this unwanted awareness of him, this sudden and totally unexpected schism in what she had believed her sexuality to be: controlled, tamed and of no real force in her life, and not what she had experienced on first seeing him.

She had gone through all the usual sexually experimental stages in her teens, but had never been promiscuous, either by inclination or peer pressure. After all, when you lived in a small town in which your father was something of a prominent figure, you felt almost honour-bound not to indulge in a variety of involvements and affairs.

In this part of the world respectability was still considered to be important and a virtue. Couples might live together, but in most cases they eventually married.

Since in the years when her peers were settling down and marrying she had had no wish to follow suit, she had chosen to remain celibate rather than indulge in a series of relationships. Rather happily celibate, if she was honest, and when she contemplated the thought of any kind of intimacy with men like Ralph Charlesworth it was revulsion that made her body shudder, not desire.

No, she had never considered herself a highly sexually motivated person, and she didn't now, which made her illogical reaction to Ben Frobisher all the more unnerving.

Had she actually, really, this afternoon, fantasised about how it would be to have him kissing her?

She did shudder now, horrified to remember just how easily and intensely she had been able to imagine what it would feel like to be taken in his arms and——

'I'll drive up to the door so that you can get out, and then I'll park the car,' her father was saying, thankfully forcing her to concentrate on the present and the blessedly mundane activity of getting out of the car.

The golf club and its course had been donated to the town in the twenties by a wealthy and benevolent local resident, who had hired an architect to design the club-house after the style of Sir Edwin Lutyens's designs for small country houses, so that it was vaguely Tudoresque in style. As the three of them went inside to wait for her father while he parked the car, Miranda acknowledged the greetings of several of her father's cronies, registering as she did so the speculative, curious looks she was getting from their wives. No need to ask herself why; the answer was standing right beside her, all six-feet-odd of manhood of him.

Why, she seethed inwardly, were there still in this day and age women who still believed that no member of their own sex could be complete without a man in her life? It was all nonsense, just the same as suggesting that no woman could be complete without having had a child. Her thoughts floundered to an uncomfortable halt as she recalled her own vulnerability in that particular direction. But then, it was not as though she considered herself incomplete without a child, it was just . . . just——

'Aunt Helen . . . not long now until the wedding, is it?'

Miranda tensed as she heard the soft hesitant voice of Susan Charlesworth, and she knew even before she had heard Ben acknowledging briefly, 'Charlesworth,' that Ralph was with her. She had almost been able to feel his presence from the atavistic reaction of her body, from the way the tiny hairs on her skin had risen in physical protest at his nearness.

It galled her unbearably sensing that Ralph was fully aware of her aversion to him and that for some reason this only caused him to increase his pursuit of her.

She didn't know how on earth poor Susan could tolerate him. In her shoes... but, then, thankfully she would never have allowed herself to be trapped in that kind of situation, married to a man who was flagrantly and frequently unfaithful, who treated her so contemptuously and inconsiderately, who humiliated her in public and, Miranda suspected, in private as well.

She was glad that her father joined them before she could be drawn into the small flood of exchanges passing between the other three as Ralph introduced his wife to Ben, and Helen explained her relationship to Susan.

Miranda excused herself on the pretext of wanting to go to the Ladies, gritting her teeth in rage and revulsion as Ralph leered at her and told her fulsomely, 'Going to check up on the old make-up, are we, then, Miranda? Shouldn't worry about too much, if I were you. A good-looking woman like you doesn't need any warpaint, although I must admit there's something about a woman's mouth when it's painted with lipstick that makes a man wonder what it would be like to kiss it off.'

As she turned her back on him, red flags of rage flying in her cheeks, Miranda heard Susan saying uncomfortably, 'Ralph! Really.'

Horrible, revolting man, Miranda seethed as she walked quickly towards the corridor and the Ladies. The language he used was almost as offensive and demeaning to her sex as the intent behind it.

As she stared at her flushed face in the mirror, she was half tempted to wipe off the discreet touch of lipstick she was wearing, but then she decided that to do so was to give in to his bullying, demeaning tactics and would allow him to see how much his words had affected her, and to a man like Ralph Charlesworth the fact that he *had* affected her, even if it was with revulsion, would be something he would consider to be a triumph.

No, she wasn't going to give him the satisfaction of seeing how much he had disgusted and offended her.

She stayed in the Ladies for as long as she could, praying that when she rejoined the others he and his wife would have left them.

When she eventually walked back into the bar, she was relieved to see that her father was in discussion with the president of the club and his wife; and that there was no sign of Ralph and Susan.

As Miranda rejoined them, Helen murmured sadly to her, 'Poor Susan; I don't know how on earth she puts up with that lout Ralph. I'm sorry if he embarrassed you, Miranda.'

'It wasn't your fault,' Miranda told her, adding, 'I can't understand why Susan stays with him either, but, then, I suppose with three children...'

'Well, yes, although she claims that she does love him.' She gave a faint sigh. 'Poor girl; I have a horrid feeling that sooner or later he's going to leave her, and that it will probably be sooner.'

Throughout the meal Ben Frobisher conversed mainly with her father. He had made several attempts to draw Miranda into their conversation, but she had resolutely refused to respond with anything more than cool politeness. The man had charm, she had to give him that, she admitted reluctantly to herself, but *she* wasn't going to be swayed by it.

Even so, she discovered that she was listening rather more intently than she would have wished when Helen questioned about his background and family.

She was surprised to discover that he was one of four children—somehow she had imagined him being an only one—and that the other three were all married with young families, something which made him the butt of a great deal of family teasing.

'You don't approve of marriage, then?' Helen hazarded, smiling at him.

He laughed. He had a nice laugh, Miranda acknowledged; it was both warm and spontaneous, crinkling his eyes at the corners and doing the most peculiar things to her insides.

'Quite the contrary,' he assured Helen, obviously not minding her questions.

'But I do believe that it's a lifetime's commitment and that as such it's something one needs to be very sure about. A marriage that is going to endure can't be based on mere sexual attraction, no matter how strong that attraction initially appears,' he said bluntly. 'That's not to say that it isn't an important part of any marriage, but it can never be the total sum of an enduring relationship. I suppose the truth is that as yet I still haven't met the woman I know I won't be able to live without.'

Helen laughed and teased him, 'I do believe you're a romantic!'

'Aren't most of us at heart?'

A computer expert who claimed to be romantic. Wasn't that a complete contradiction?

'Are *you* a romantic, Miranda?'

She stared at him, and felt her skin starting to flush. His question had caught her off guard. She had been listening to the conversation and yet had considered herself safely outside it. Now she wondered if he hadn't thrown the question at her because he wanted to embarrass her, rather than through any desire to know what motivated her.

'Miranda, romantic?' her father snorted, answering the question for her. 'Miranda is one of your modern breed of women who scorns such old-fashioned notions. She prides herself on being independent and self-sufficient.'

Miranda knew that her father was really only teasing her, but for some reason his words hurt her, drawing a picture of her which her emotions instantly rejected as she viewed the cold, emotionless creature his words had created. She wasn't really like that, was she?

It was true that she *was* independent, but that was because... because... because what? Because she had wanted to give her father his freedom... his right to have a life of his own, the kind of life he might not have felt free to have with an adult daughter still living under his roof.

Well, maybe her motivation hadn't been quite so altruistic, and certainly she enjoyed her work, but, if she was truly the woman her father seemed to think, wouldn't she have long ago left this small market town behind her and headed out into a much wider and harsher world?

'Jeffrey, honestly, that's not true,' Helen intervened. 'Don't listen to him, Ben,' she exhorted. 'Miranda might try to hide it, but in reality she's one of the most tender-hearted people you could ever wish to meet, although I know she hates admitting it. I suspect she's rather afraid of letting people see how tender-hearted she actually is in case it makes her too vulnerable.'

Miranda was horrified. Much as she had disliked her father's jocular misrepresentation of her as a hard-headed determined woman with no room in her life for time-wasting emotions, it had been preferable to Helen's far too accurate portrait of her.

She knew that Ben Frobisher was looking at her, but she could not bring herself to return his look with anything like the composure that doing so required.

'No one likes to appear too vulnerable,' she could hear him saying, but, although the words were addressed to Helen, she could sense that he was still watching her.

Her appetite had deserted her completely. She pushed the food around on her plate, longing for the evening to be over. She had been right; the only thing she had not guessed was the true intensity of the evening's awfulness.

She was glad when her father started to ask Ben about his plans for relocating his business to the town, and was both surprised and rather chagrined to learn that, while he would be bringing some key people down with him from London, he was hoping to recruit the majority of his employees locally.

'It's the kind of business that requires young sharp minds,' he told them all. 'At a recent convention, the majority of those attending were under thirty, and a good percentage were under twenty. At the moment we hold a good place in the market because we've been able to specialise in a profitable area, but we can only hold on to that advantage if we remain in the forefront of new advances, and in order to do that we need keen, innovative minds.'

'What will happen to your existing employees?' Miranda asked him.

'Most of them have already found new jobs. There's no shortage of demand for trained people in and around London, and, of course, they're all getting redundancy payments. In fact, none of them actually wanted to relocate with us. They're all under thirty, with established lifestyles in London, most of them are unmarried, and the thought of moving out to a quiet market town didn't have much appeal for them.'

'But it did for you?'

Miranda had no idea why she was questioning him...talking to him. If she had any sense she would simply sit here in silence, having as little to do with him as possible.

'I'm not under thirty. The pace of London life doesn't have much appeal for me any more. I wanted a home...not a glossy London flat that's antiseptic and arid. I've always liked this part of the world. My parents lived near Bath for a while when I was in my teens. They've moved north now. My father comes from the Borders and wanted to go back there when he retired.'

'Which reminds me,' her father interrupted. 'I've got the details of some houses for you. You did say you'd prefer something outside the town?'

'Yes, I do.'

While the two men discussed the various properties available, Helen commented to Miranda that she would be glad when all the fuss of the wedding was over.

Everyone had finished eating, coffee had been served, and the moment Miranda had been privately dreading had arrived.

The lights had been dimmed, the small band had started playing and couples were gradually filling the dance floor.

She prayed that Ben would not out of politeness ask her to dance. The very last thing she wanted was to be held in his arms. And yet, what had she to fear? She had already convinced herself that, no matter how physically attractive she had originally found him, that attraction had vanished once she knew who and what he was, and, that being the case, what had she to fear from dancing with him? Nothing; nothing at all, and anyway, why was she inviting problems that might not occur? In all probability he wasn't even going to invite her to dance with him.

# CHAPTER THREE

'WOULD you like to dance?'

Miranda tensed. How could she refuse?

'Er—thank you.'

Unsteadily she stood up and allowed Ben Frobisher to guide her towards the dance floor.

'I'm sorry if this evening has rather lumbered you with me,' he apologised to her. 'When your father asked me to join him this evening, I thought it might be a good way of getting to know a few people.'

Miranda tried not to think about the effect his proximity was having on her. Treat him just like any other client you've had to entertain, she exhorted herself, but she knew already that that was impossible.

The band was playing a waltz, and her body tensed involuntarily as Ben took her in his arms.

'It's hard to believe that the waltz was once banned for being decadent, isn't it?' she said breathlessly as she fought to dismiss the sensations invoked by his touch, sensations which were making her feel as nervous and ill at ease as a teenager. Thank goodness it was impossible for him to know just how he was affecting her!

'Oh, I don't know,' he responded thoughtfully, 'when you bear in mind that it was the first time that men and women had actually danced exclusively with one partner and the opportunities it affords for body contact. And even these days it isn't exactly unknown for couples to take advantage of the intimacy allowed in dancing together to reinforce their desire for one another.'

She couldn't help it—her skin went hot as her mind treacherously conjured up a mental image of the two of *them* swaying intimately together, dancing body to body, his arms wrapped around her so that she was aware of every movement of his muscles, every breath he took, every small reaction of his flesh to hers... She trembled uncontrollably, causing him to frown down at her and enquire in concern, 'Are you cold?'

'Yes. Just a little,' she lied. It wasn't true; if anything she was too hot, but she could hardly admit to him just what had caused that sensual *frisson* of sensation to galvanise her body.

As she matched her steps to his she had an appalling urge to move nearer to him, to close the gap between their bodies and to...

Desperately she shut her eyes, trying to suppress the illicit wash of sensation that rushed through her, but the darkness only made things worse, only increased her sensual awareness of him to the pitch where she was as intimately aware of the heat and scent of him as though they were in fact established lovers.

That shook her more than anything else—that ready acceptance of her senses to acknowledge her physical responsiveness to him.

That was the trouble with being a daydreamer, with having a far too vivid imagination, she told herself bitterly. It led you into all sorts of dangerous assumptions.

For example, if she hadn't given in this afternoon to her own idiotic and wanton impulse to tamper with the actual reality of her earlier brief meeting with him, transforming it into some kind of impossible erotic encounter, she would not be suffering the humiliation and discomfort of trying to subdue her body's physical response to him right now.

Thank God that as yet no one had developed any means of correctly reading the human mind. The very last thing she could have endured would have been the ignominy of knowing that he had guessed what was happening to her.

She tried to convince herself that in these days of equality it was no more shameful to her as a woman that she should be so physically affected by a man she hardly knew, and who had definitely not given her any encouragement to feel that desire, than had their positions been reversed, but it didn't work.

She was obviously a good deal more gender-orientated than she had supposed, she reflected wryly.

'Your father was telling me that you live out at Gallows Reach.'

The soft-voiced comment made her stiffen slightly before admitting, 'Yes, I have a cottage out there.'

'You don't find it too remote?'

'Not really. Perhaps if I weren't mixing with so many people during the day I might find it too isolated, but as it is...'

'Mmm. I know what you mean. I must say, I'm enjoying the solitude of the place I'm renting. I thought it would be a good idea to see how I took to living somewhere so remote before I actually took the plunge and bought a property.'

'And how are you finding it?' Miranda asked him curiously.

'Interesting,' he told her promptly. 'Something of a voyage of self-discovery, in fact. It's rather a long time since I've spent so much time on my own.'

Miranda tensed again. Did that mean that, despite the fact that he wasn't married, there was or had been someone important in his life? But his next words disproved this theory, as he added, 'In London I had an apartment at the top of the building which housed our office. Not an ideal situation because it meant that I was virtually spending twenty-four hours a day with my work. In the beginning when we first set up in business that was necessary, but recently I've began to find that my whole life seems to revolve around the company.'

Miranda gave a tiny shrug. 'If you want to succeed these days, you have to be prepared to devote the major part of your time to your career.'

'And is that what you want? To put your career before everything else in your life?'

'No, it isn't. If it was I'd be working in London, not here. I like my work. I enjoy the independence it gives me, but I enjoy other things as well.'

'Such as?'

His question surprised her into focusing on him. He was watching her closely, the grey eyes alert and thoughtful, the mouth... She gulped and swallowed hard as her gaze slipped inadvertently to his mouth and stayed there as though hypnotised.

'I...I...I enjoy all sorts of things,' she told him huskily, adding mentally to herself, yes, dangerous things such as cuddling friends' babies and day-dreaming about strangers.

'Your father was telling me that you're actively involved in several local committees.'

'Er—yes.'

'Including a newly formed one to protect the town's historic buildings,' he probed.

'That's right,' Miranda agreed, wondering where his questions were leading.

'Charlesworth seems to think that your committee is trying to stir up local opposition to the expansion and redevelopment of the town, even when that expansion would quite clearly be to the benefit of the local inhabitants.'

'Like your new offices?' Miranda queried drily, her desire for him thankfully subdued by her anger at what was being allowed to happen to the town.

'Surely it would have been possible to site your offices outside the town, in a purpose-built unit designed to house all the modern hi-tech equipment you might need, rather than despoiling what was a perfect example of small-town Georgian architecture? Too many of our towns are losing their character, their links with the past, to provide anonymous ugly homes for businesses which demand that their environment be destroyed... an environment which could have existed quite happily for several hundred years, and for what? To provide space for a business or a shop which might be in existence for less than a couple of years. It's insane and——'

'I quite agree, which is why...'

He stopped speaking as the band stopped playing, leaving Miranda to flush uncomfortably and guiltily as she realised how carried away she had been by her own principles and beliefs.

'I'm sorry, but it's a subject I feel very strongly about,' she apologised stiffly, all too conscious of the amused look he was giving her.

'So I perceive,' he agreed, adding softly, 'Tell me, what else arouses those strong emotions of yours?'

Miranda gave him a suspicious look. If she had received that kind of comment from anyone else, she might have suspected them of trying to flirt with her, but there was nothing flirtatious in the way he was looking at her.

'I ask simply so that I can avoid treading on any dangerous ground,' he told her calmly.

'I feel strongly about a good many issues,' she told him coldly. 'But, since they can hardly be of any interest to you, I don't see much point in discussing them.'

Without waiting for him to follow her, she started to walk back towards their table, but he caught up with her almost immediately, and as he slipped his hand beneath her elbow to escort her off the floor she thought she heard him saying under his breath, 'You'd be surprised.'

\* \* \*

He was probably only probing into her work with the committee to preserve the town's historic buildings because of the work he was having done on the house he had bought, Miranda decided ten minutes later when she was still mentally mulling over their conversation. She was alone at the table, her father having gone over to chat to the president and his wife, and Ben having asked Helen to dance.

It was hot in the ballroom, and she decided to take advantage of the fact that she was alone by slipping out of the room to get some fresh air.

It was possible to walk from the club-house around the building and re-enter it through the conservatory, which had been added to the rear to provide somewhere for the ladies to enjoy their afternoon tea undisturbed by the men.

It was that kind of golf club, and so far none of the members seemed inclined to object to this seg-regation of the sexes.

It was cool outside, cooler in fact than she had thought, and she shivered a little, walking more quickly. Although the front of the club-house was illuminated, the side was shadowed, the darkness somehow vaguely threatening. Ahead of her she could see the lights of the conservatory. The door was open as though others had had the same idea as herself and used it to seek some fresh air.

Perhaps because she was concentrating on other things, she had no awareness of anyone coming up behind her until she was grabbed from behind and a leering and unwelcome familiar voice was saying in her ear, 'Well, now, isn't this just a piece of luck?

It isn't often I get the chance to get you all to myself.'

Ralph Charlesworth. Miranda stiffened immediately, trying to quell the panicky disgust that threatened to overwhelm her at being touched by him.

'Let me go, Ralph,' she demanded through gritted teeth.

'Well, now, you're going to have to ask me a good deal more nicely than that,' he taunted her.

He was standing far too close to her, dragging her back against his body, and holding her there with one hand while the other stroked through her hair and down the side of her throat, causing her to shudder in revulsion.

'You know I've wanted you for one hell of a long time, Miranda. Why don't you stop fighting it and try being nice to me? I'm a generous man ... both as a lover and as a man, if you know what I mean.'

Sickness boiled in her stomach, but she fought it down. If she panicked now ... She cringed inwardly, knowing how much he would enjoy her terror. Men like him always did ... they enjoyed hurting women ... bullying them.

She prayed that someone else would come along the path and afford her an opportunity to escape. The hand which had been caressing her throat had now reached her shoulder and she realised in horror that within another few seconds he would probably be touching her breast.

She could feel the sweat breaking out on her body at the thought and repeated angrily, 'Ralph, let me go. You're a married man...remember?' she added desperately.

'Is that all that's stopping you?' He almost crooned the words as though scenting victory. 'Susie won't mind. In fact, she'll be grateful to you,' he told her, trying to turn her in his arms. 'She doesn't like sex, my wife doesn't. She's only too glad if someone else keeps me out of her bed. I should never have married her. I *wouldn't* have married her if she hadn't damn well gone and got herself pregnant.'

Anger and revulsion burned nauseously in Miranda's throat.

'I didn't think that was possible, Ralph,' she challenged him acidly. 'For a woman to get *herself* pregnant, I mean.'

He laughed. 'Well, don't go worrying about it. By the time a man gets to my age he knows a thing or two. *You* won't have any worries in that direction. Anyway, I expect you're on the Pill, aren't you? All you modern women——'

'Ralph, let me go!' she demanded for the third time.

'Oh, come on, you can't fool me,' he interrupted her. 'You might have given me the cold shoulder, but underneath... Well, why don't you admit it? You want it as much as I do.'

He added something so degrading and coarse that Miranda could actually feel the blood draining out of her face.

Quite what would have happened if they hadn't heard someone coming down the path behind them and Ralph hadn't momentarily released her, she dreaded to think.

As luck would have it, the other couple were close friends of her father's and she was able to escape from Ralph by firmly attaching herself to them.

To her relief, Ralph made no attempt to follow her, and it was only when she was safely back inside that she was able to admit to herself how truly frightened she had been. It seemed almost hysterical to frame the word 'rape' even in her own mind, but she had no doubt as to what Ralph had had in mind, and it most certainly would not have happened with her consent.

She went into the Ladies more to gain time to calm down a little than for any other reason. In the mirror she saw that her face was pale, her eyes wide and dark with fear.

She combed her hair and retouched her lipstick, and then squared her shoulders and stepped back out into the corridor.

She was halfway down it when she became aware that someone was behind, following her. A hand touched her arm, and immediately she panicked, turning round abruptly and hissing fiercely, 'Look, I've already told you, Ralph. I'm not interested. In fact you——' She stopped abruptly as she realised that it wasn't Ralph behind her but Ben, her face going scarlet with mortification.

She saw that he was frowning, his expression almost harsh as he took hold of her arm and drew her firmly into a shadowy alcove.

'What's wrong?' he asked her curtly. 'Is Charlesworth bothering you?'

Miranda bit her lip. She had never felt so mortified in all her life. Of all the people to discover . . .

'This doesn't concern you,' she told him huskily. 'And if you'd just let go of my arm, I'd like to rejoin my father . . .'

'In a minute, and as for it not concerning me . . . was it *Charlesworth* you were running away from earlier today when you bumped into me?'

His perception dismayed her. She tried to frame a convincing lie and found that instead she was saying shakily and wretchedly, 'What if it was? Look, I'm an adult, not a child, and I'm perfectly capable of making clear to a man that his . . . his interest isn't wanted.'

'Are you?' The dry disbelief in his voice made her wince. 'It doesn't look like it from where I stand.' He paused for a moment, and Miranda was conscious of him watching her, assessing her almost, she suspected, and then he said quietly, 'Look, let's forget that you've decided that you and I are on opposite sides of an uncrossable chasm for the moment, shall we? All right, so this is none of my business, but if you genuinely don't want Charlesworth——'

Miranda's outraged gasp silenced him.

'I'm not sure *what* you're insinuating,' she hissed angrily, 'but I can assure you that I have absolutely no interest whatsoever in Ralph. Apart from the fact that he's married, I think he's the most . . . the most revolting example of the male sex I've ever met!'

'Well, that seems definite enough.'

Was he actually daring to laugh at her? Miranda stared up at him. There was humour in his voice, but it wasn't mirrored in his eyes.

'Look,' he said almost gently, 'there is a type of man, personified by the Charlesworths of this world, who seem to believe that when a woman says "no", no matter how determinedly she says it, what she's really doing is encouraging them to prove her wrong. I'm afraid that your rejection of him is only going to make him all the more determined in his pursuit of you.'

Miranda's heart sank. Ben Frobisher was only telling her what she had already come to believe herself, but it was a confirmation she would rather not have had.

'So, what am I supposed to do?' she demanded warily. 'Tell him "yes", in the hope that he'll lose interest?'

'No. But there is a third solution. I suspect that if Charlesworth thought you weren't interested in him because you were involved with someone else, he'd soon back off. Men like him enjoy bullying women, but when it comes to their own sex they tend to be a little more wary.'

'Yes . . . you're probably right,' Miranda agreed, 'but since I'm *not* involved with anyone else . . .'

The shock of what had happened was just beginning to sink in, making her snappy and edgy. Her tension showed in her voice, but she didn't care. All she wanted to do right now was to go home where she could be safe and alone.

'I think possibly you mean that you *weren't*,' Ben Frobisher informed her thoughtfully.

He was standing facing her, looking down the corridor, and as he spoke she sensed that he was focusing on something or someone behind her, but only a small part of her brain registered this fact, the rest of it being busy getting ready to refute his extraordinary statement.

However, before she could do so, to her utter disbelief, for the second time that evening she found herself held hard by a pair of male arms as Ben took hold of her, not roughly as Ralph had done, but gently, tenderly almost, she realised as she grappled with her shock; more as a lover would have done than an aggressor. And it seemed that her body too sensed that difference, so that when Ben drew her firmly against him it had no compulsion to resist the pressure of the hands which lingeringly moulded her body to his before one of them settled in the small of her back while the other slid beneath her hair to caress her nape and then her jaw, sliding against her skin, tilting her head, bending his own, his face completely in the shadows, so that she could see nothing of his expression, only the brief gleam of his eyes catching her gaze and holding it transfixed, in much the same way as the total unexpectedness of his actions had transfixed her brain, paralysing her ability to think or reason.

When he brushed her lips slowly with his own, once, twice and then a third time, she couldn't fight the compulsion to close her eyes, to move closer to him, to cling to the soft pressure of his mouth, stilling its tormenting movements. She made a soft sound of pleasure when his mouth remained on her own, and then quivered slightly as he framed her face with both his hands, and then kissed her slowly and deliberately, taking his time over the exercise, lingering over it, as though the softness of her mouth beneath his own was a sensation, a warmth, a pleasure he couldn't bear to relinquish.

The simple sensual pleasure of being kissed so gently and yet so erotically was so shockingly intense and unexpected that Miranda completely forgot that this was a stranger kissing her; a man who while she might initially have found him physically attractive, was someone with whom, not so very long ago, she had felt completely at odds.

All she knew was that the way he was kissing her, the way he was holding her, the response he was arousing within her were so very different from anything she had ever experienced before, so illuminatingly pleasurable, that she never wanted him to let her go.

And yet that was exactly what he did, gently easing his mouth away from hers, and then, although still holding her, slowly moved away from her body so that she shivered as she felt the chill of the night air touching her warmly aroused flesh.

Reluctantly she opened her eyes and focused on him. What had happened had been so unexpected, so uninvited. Could he, like her, have felt that same *frisson* of awareness, of desire when they had first met? Had for some reason her disclosures about the unwanted attention of Ralph Charlesworth compelled Ben to break all the rules of convention and take the risk of kissing her?

But, even as these wild incoherent thoughts whirled through her mind, Ben had started to speak, apologising gravely as he told her, 'I'm sorry if I startled you, pouncing on you like that, but it seemed too good an opportunity to miss. After what you'd been telling me, I saw Charlesworth watching us . . . well, as I said, I suspect he's the kind of man who, although he might not hesitate to try and bully a woman, will quickly back off if he thinks there's another man involved.'

*That* was why he had kissed her!

Reality, so very different from her foolish imaginings, was like a shock of cold water, not only immediately dousing the desire she had been feeling but also turning the soft warm feeling of well-being and happiness inside her to one of seething bitter resentment, as she reflected angrily on the humiliation she could well have suffered if *she* had been the one to speak first; if *she* had allowed him to see that the kiss, which he had instigated purely as a counter-measure to Ralph Charlesworth's desire for her, had been something which she had mistaken as physical evidence that he shared the attraction she had felt the first time she had seen him.

It was mortification and not embarrassment that turned her face red and made her step back from him, but fortunately he didn't seem to be aware of it, apologising briefly, 'I'm sorry . . . but there just wasn't any time to warn you. I saw Charlesworth watching us.'

'Yes,' Miranda intervened, now as eager to escape from him as she had been earlier from Ralph, although for very different reasons.

'Well, let's hope it does the trick,' Ben told her. 'I hadn't realised he was such an unsavoury character,' he added, frowning slightly. 'His wife is connected to Helen?'

'Yes, her niece. Yes,' Miranda agreed shortly. How could he stand there and calmly discuss something as mundane as Helen's relationship to Susan Charlesworth when she...? She gritted her teeth, acknowledging that she was still having trouble functioning on a normal plane. Her mind might have realised that there had been nothing personal in Ben's kiss, but her body, her senses...they were being extraordinarily recalcitrant and rebellious about doing so. They were still clinging dreamily to the pleasure he had given them.

'I think we'd better go and rejoin your father. He'll be wondering where we are.'

Privately Miranda doubted it, but she allowed Ben to head her back towards the others. He obviously didn't want to spend any more time alone with her than he had to.

As they re-entered the ballroom, the first person Miranda saw was Ralph Charlesworth. He was standing with a small group of people, and as she and Ben walked past them Miranda could feel him glowering at her.

She couldn't bring herself to look at Ben, although she knew from the way he drew her imperceptibly closer to her side that he too was aware of him.

As they headed for their table she wondered shakily how it was that her body should have become so aware of him in such a very short space of time that it had actually reacted to the closing of that small conventional gap between them—the gap that said they were acquaintances and not lovers—by becoming dangerously fluid and soft, as though her flesh actually yearned for physical contact with his.

All in all, Miranda was glad when the evening had finally come to an end, and she was free to escape to the solitary security of her own home, having firmly refused to join Helen, her father and Ben in a final cup of coffee before they finally declared the evening ended.

# CHAPTER FOUR

MIRANDA woke up, tensing in the warm darkness of her bed, until she realised that the sound which had awakened her was just the wind.

It was still dark, her alarm showing that it was just gone three in the morning.

She had been in bed for just over an hour, and now she moved restlessly beneath the bedclothes, reluctant to admit that it wasn't so much the sound of the wind which had woken her but the dream she had been having.

She shivered a little, sitting up in bed and hugging her arms around her knees. Her dream had been so real that just for a moment when she had first opened her eyes she had been shocked to discover that Ben Frobisher wasn't actually with her.

Ben Frobisher. Drat the wretched man. Wasn't it enough that he had already invaded her conscious life without him invading her subconscious and her dreams as well?

And now, instead of closing her eyes and going back to sleep, she was sitting here half-afraid to do so just in case she started the dream again.

The dream. She tensed and swallowed. It had been so real...so...so wantonly erotic, a small voice whispered tauntingly. Despite the fact that she was completely alone, she knew that she was blushing.

61

With anger, not embarrassment, she told herself sharply, but it wasn't entirely true. If she closed her eyes, would she once again find herself in Ben Frobisher's arms, being kissed as he had kissed her in reality earlier in the evening, only this time...?

She tensed again but it was too late to head off her rebellious thoughts. Even without closing her eyes she could recall it all so vividly, the sensation of being held in Ben's arms; the heat and power of his body against hers, the delicious *frisson* of sensation that raced over her skin as her body yielded instinctively to the sensual demand of his.

The soft brush of his lips against hers, a tantalising preliminary to the pleasure she knew was to come, was teasingly provocative and yet held a promise that lured her deeper and deeper into the enmeshing need he was feeding inside her.

In her dream there had been no reason for her to resist the warm ardour of his mouth; no need to warn herself that it would be folly to allow herself to feel such intense desire.

In her dream it had seemed the most natural thing in the world to wind her arms around his neck; to slide her fingers into the thick darkness of his hair and to tighten them against his scalp in a reflex acknowledgement of the emotion gripping her as her touch caused him to deepen their kiss, to hold her so close to his body that she could actually feel the reverberation within her own flesh of his unsteady heartbeat.

In her dream—and this was what disturbed and alarmed her—the kiss had not finished as it had done in reality, with Ben stepping back from her and calmly explaining that he had kissed her, not because he desired her, but to help her evade Ralph Charlesworth's unwanted attention. Instead, Ben had continued to kiss her with increasing urgency; an urgency to which she had shamelessly and wantonly responded, allowing him to see how much he was arousing her.

In her dream, when he had reluctantly released her mouth, he had kissed the smooth line of her jaw and then the tender vulnerable spot behind her ear, slowly caressing the entire length of her throat so that she trembled violently against him, suppressing her soft moans of pleasure, twisting feverishly against him as his mouth caressed the soft skin of her shoulder, pushing aside the fabric of her dress as he kissed the hollow above her collarbone and then bit passionately, roughly almost, at her skin as though unable to control his need for her any longer.

It had been at that point that she had woken up with her heart beating frantically and her body soft and moist with desire for him.

And now she was afraid to go back to sleep. Afraid in case she started dreaming about him again, but it was only three o'clock in the morning and she was desperately tired. Perhaps if she willed herself not to think about him, but to concentrate on something else instead . . . such as her work . . . such as the coming wedding . . . anything . . . anything at all that would put her in touch with reality and keep at bay her wanton disruptive dreams.

\* \* \*

'I'm sorry,' Miranda apologised, smothering a yawn as she listened to her father describing a new property he had taken on to their books. 'I didn't get much sleep last night.'

And whose fault had that been? Miranda reflected bitterly half an hour later as she started to clear her desk, ready for going home. Certainly not hers. If she had been afraid to let herself relax enough to sleep properly last night because she had been afraid of dreaming about Ben Frobisher again, it had been his fault and not hers. After all, *she* had not been the one who had instigated that kiss...*she* had not invited it nor encouraged it.

But she had enjoyed and totally misunderstood it, she reminded herself grimly as she left the office and got into her car.

Face it, she told herself bluntly, either you've got some kind of compulsion to start behaving like a teenager again, or you're seriously vulnerable to the man.

Of the two she thought she preferred the first option, but common sense told her that she was far more likely to be suffering from the latter.

So, what was she trying to tell herself? she demanded mentally as she started her car and set it in motion.

That she had fallen in love with Ben Frobisher? Ridiculous. Impossible. Totally unthinkable. There must be some other, more logical and acceptable reason for her extraordinary reaction to him.

Yes, it was quite impossible for her to have fallen in love with Ben; for a start, it was simply not the sort of thing she did; she was far too sensible.

All she needed to do was to find the reason, but not right now: for one thing, she was far too tired, and, for another, she already had far too many other things to do.

Reassuring herself that she wasn't being a coward and evading the issue, she reminded herself that tonight she was due to attend a meeting of the newly established preservation society, which meant that she was barely going to have time to get home, have something to eat, and get showered and changed again before it was time to go out.

As her father would no doubt have reminded her, had he been with her, if she had done the sensible thing and bought herself a comfortable small house close to the town, as he had wanted her to do, she would not have to waste so much time in travelling.

But then, she had fallen in love with the cottage the moment she had seen it.

She put her foot on the brake so sharply that she jolted forward in her seat, and then realised as she stared in bewilderment at the empty road that her physical reaction had been caused by the sub-conscious danger of her thoughts. If she had fallen in love at first sight with the cottage, then . . .

But that was something completely different, she told herself quickly as she drove homeward. She might have allowed herself the indulgence of buying the cottage for reasons which were emotionally based rather than practical, but that did not necessarily mean to say that she was . . . that she could . . . While her thoughts floundered into hopeless disorder she wondered a little wildly if it was being so close to the threshold of entering her thirties that was responsible for this apparent up-heaval and complete turn-around in her emotions and convictions.

First she started going all broody and cooing over other people's babies, then . . .

Stop it, she warned herself. Stop it right now. Stop those thoughts right there before . . .

Before what? Before it was too late and she had allowed herself to commit the unutterable folly of actually allowing a bridge to connect her newly emergent desire for motherhood with her emotional and physical vulnerability to Ben Frobisher.

But of course she was not going to be stupid enough to allow that to happen. Of course she wasn't, a mocking inner voice taunted her. Of course she wasn't.

As she herself had predicted, she barely had time to snatch a quick snack before it was time to get ready to go out again.

As yet the newly formed society had no permanent home, but the wife of the landlord of the town's fifteenth-century coaching inn, who was one of their members, had offered the use of a room above the main bar as a temporary meeting place.

The coaching inn, like so many other buildings in the town, had come under threat from the new developments. The small brewery which owned it had recently been taken over by a large national group which specialised in turning the majority of their public houses into standardised steak houses of the cheap and cheerful controlled portions variety, which, while they might suit the needs and demands of the busy traveller and his family, had little aesthetic appeal.

As she drove into what had originally been the stable area and coaching yard, Miranda noticed that she was already five minutes late and cursed under her breath. The car park was almost full and it took her a further five minutes to park, and, when she eventually hurried up the stairs to the meeting room, she was hot and slightly breathless.

As she opened the door an expectant hush seized the people inside, causing her to pause for a moment, until the chairwoman greeted her, saying, 'Oh, Miranda, it's only you; for a moment we thought... You'll never guess what,' she added, 'the most marvellous thing. You know the house that's being renovated in the High Street, the one we were all so concerned about when we heard it had been bought by a computer firm? Well, the person who's bought it—a Mr Frobisher—phoned me this afternoon. Apparently he had to get my number from the local library. We really must think about putting a notice in the local rag, you know. I mean it was obviously only by chance that he'd discovered we existed at all. Anyway, it turns out that he'd heard of our concern about what's happening to so many of our fine old buildings, and he wanted to reassure us that he had no intention of destroying the character of the house he's bought. In fact, he actually offered to come down here tonight to show us all the plans for the building. I was so thrilled...I mean, this shows how important our work is, doesn't it? And to have got such a good response... I must say, I felt really heartened. I've already told the others. We half expected when you walked in that you would be Mr Frobisher. If only others can be persuaded to follow his good example.'

'We don't know as yet that his *will* be a good example,' Miranda pointed out grimly.

She could tell that the others were surprised by her response and its lack of enthusiasm, but how could she tell them what she suspected—that a man like Ben Frobisher would simply use them, flattering them into acceptance of a design she was pretty sure would ruin the authenticity of the building? Oh, he would flatter them, charm them, use all the knowledge and sophistication at his command to ensure that he had their approval, and she knew already that there would be nothing *she* could do about it; but why was he bothering? He already had planning permission for the work he was having done. Or was he perhaps contemplating expanding... buying further properties?

The anger and apprehension she felt was intensified by a feeling almost of having been betrayed... a feeling that somehow or other he had gone behind her back, and yet in contacting the chairwoman of their committee he had behaved completely correctly.

But he could have told her what he intended to do... could have warned her... That way...

That way what? That way she would have found some way of avoiding attending the meeting... But then, *he* was hardly likely to know of any reason why she might wish to avoid him, was he? No doubt he probably even considered her indebted to him for rescuing her from Ralph. And perhaps in a way she was. She suspected that he had been quite correct in guessing that Ralph would cease pestering her if he thought that, instead of having to browbeat and bully a woman, he was going to have to confront another man. Ralph's attitude to women epitomised everything she most resented and disliked in the male sex, she acknowledged tiredly as she took her place at the large table around which they held their meetings.

'What time did he say he would be here?' she heard one of the others asking the chairwoman.

'Well, I suggested he leave it until a quarter to nine to give everyone time to arrive, so he should be here any minute now.' She glanced at her watch as she spoke, and, as though on cue, someone rapped firmly on the door and then opened it.

Since Miranda had been told of Ben's imminent arrival, it seemed scarcely necessary for her heart to start beating as frantically as though it had just received a sudden shock, she told herself irritably as she deliberately refused to do anything more than briefly acknowledge his presence with a small inclination of her head, leaving it to Alice Thornton, their chairwoman, to go forward and welcome him.

He was carrying a roll of paper: the much-vaunted plans, no doubt.

Alice Thornton was in her early sixties, the old-fashioned, rather formal type who, as Miranda had known she would, insisted on making Ben personally known to all of them. Whether by accident or as a gentle reproof because *she* had been

late, Miranda had no idea, but somehow or other
she was the last to be introduced to him, but before
she could say anything he was smiling at her and
saying warmly, 'Oh, Miranda and I already know
one another,' and, as they all sat down, Miranda
was forced to make a response to her neighbour's
excited questions.

'You know him? How did you meet? Is he
married, do you know, or...?'

Reminding herself that this kind of direct
questioning was one of the penalties one paid for
living in a small town and for having a father who
was known to almost every single one of its long-
standing inhabitants, she answered her neighbour's
questions as quickly as she could, explaining that
they had met through her father, adding as coolly
as she dared that as far as she knew Ben was not
married.

'He's very good-looking,' her interrogator said
wistfully. She was a small quiet woman in her late
forties, who to Miranda's knowledge had been contentedly and happily married to her husband for
twenty-odd years, and so this response caused
Miranda to repeat to herself her own earlier
warnings about the dangers of allowing herself to
become vulnerable to the allure of surface looks
and facile charm.

The chairwoman was standing up, commanding
their attention, announcing that Mr Frobisher had
kindly suggested coming along to allay their fears
about the conversion of the house he had bought
in the High Street, and that for this purpose he had
brought with him his plans.

Though he thanked her with an ease that suggested that he was not unfamiliar with public speaking—even if the warmth in his voice *did* suggest that it was a special pleasure to be with them in a way that Miranda told herself she could only despise because it meant that he was deliberately trying to charm and befuddle them—no doubt while he was talking to them he would be secretly laughing at them, amused by their small-townness and amateurish approach. But at least *they* were genuine in their emotions and beliefs, she thought irefully, while he...

He was spreading the plans out on the table, making it necessary for them to crowd closer together in order to see them.

As she listened to him pointing out where special features were being retained, even at the expense of convenience and cost, she tried not to admit how much she enjoyed listening to his voice.

'Miranda, you can't possibly see from there,' Bob Voysey, their treasurer, whispered fussily.

Bob was a bachelor of around her father's age, who, until her death three years ago, had lived with his mother. One of Miranda's friends had gigglingly suggested that she suspected he had a crush on Miranda and that she'd better watch out if she didn't want to take his mother's place in his life.

Miranda hadn't been amused. She liked Bob and felt a little sorry for him in his obvious loneliness, but ever since hearing that light-hearted comment she had taken good care to make sure that she treated him with a formal distance that made it plain that, while she respected and liked him, she considered him to be a member of an older generation in whom she had no romantic interest.

Now as he whispered to her she flushed, more out of an awareness that Ben had focused on them and was watching them, his attention no doubt drawn to them by Bob's whisper, than because she was embarrassed at not being able to see the plans.

'Oh, that's all right,' Ben smiled. 'I've already arranged to show Miranda the plans. In fact, that's what gave me the idea of coming here to see you all tonight. When we were out the other night, Miranda made it so plain to me how much concern there is locally about the way in which so many of your older buildings are being destroyed that I wanted to come here myself to set your minds at rest where my building at least is concerned.'

Furious with him for implying, even if unintentionally, that their relationship was far more intimate than it ever was or could be, and knowing how eagerly and enthusiastically this snippet of information would be passed around the town, duly garnished and embellished, Miranda gritted her teeth and all but snapped at him.

'Yes, but isn't it a fact that, where computers are concerned, equipment needs to be housed at certain static temperatures and in certain stable conditions which will mean that the interior of the building will virtually have to be ripped out?'

'Yes, that is true,' Ben agreed evenly. 'But since *we* are concerned with producing and writing software, and not computers, the excellent cellars beneath the building are ideal for conversion for that purpose.'

Miranda knew she was flushing again. This time with anger. He was making her look a complete fool, she thought bitterly.

As though he had read her mind, Ben continued quietly, 'I have to admit, though, that your point is a valid one, and that one of the reasons I bought that particular house was to overcome the problems of housing modern computer equipment in an old building.'

'In that case, why not use a purpose-built complex somewhere outside the town?' Miranda suggested grittily.

The smile he gave her made her stomach muscles quiver. Sternly quelling such rebelliousness, she refused to respond to it, fixing her gaze on a point just over his shoulder, wishing desperately that she had never opened this argument, but stubbornly knowing that now that she had she wasn't going to back down.

'Computer programmers are human too, you know,' Ben responded wryly. 'They are as vulnerable as the rest of society to their surroundings. I'm afraid it is a myth that all of them want to live, eat, sleep and work in the kind of minimalistic and arid atmosphere beloved of certain glossy magazines.

'In theory, no doubt, there are those who do actually enjoy living and working in a stark white room, broken up by two or three pieces of carefully chosen and very uncomfortable-looking black furniture, but I rather suspect that the majority of my employees would have something very unpleasant to say to me if I tried suggesting they work in that kind of hi-tech environment.

'As a matter of fact, my secretary has already informed me that if a black leather settee or chair dares to put in an appearance anywhere in the building, she and the rest of the staff will go on strike.'

There was a small pause while everyone laughed and the tension that had begun to grip them eased.

When it came to gamesmanship, he was a master player, Miranda reflected sourly. He had the others eating out of the palm of his hand. Another half an hour or so of his skilled verbal manipulation and they would be praising him as the vanguard of a new kind of environmentally conscious and considerate businessman. They might even start proposing giving him a medal for it. Well she wasn't going to be hoodwinked and soothed into complacency. She knew the kind of work Ralph Charlesworth did.

Compressing her mouth, she lifted her chin and demanded coldly, 'You state that you are anxious to conserve the character of the building, and yet the contractor undertaking the work for you is notor—— well-known for his belief that anything over ten years old should be razed to the ground.'

Miranda could hear the stunned gasps from the other members of the committee. No matter how much they all might disapprove of what Ralph Charlesworth was doing, no matter how much they might carefully and in low whispers and only among themselves criticise him for it, it simply was not done to voice those views out loud, especially not in front of an outsider... an incomer. Ralph was after all one of their own.

'Yes, I'm glad you raised that,' Ben responded quietly, silencing not only the gasps of the others, but the impulsive torrent of words she had been about to utter as well.

She stared at him, too taken aback to speak, thus giving him the advantage to continue.

'I have, in fact, engaged another firm of contractors, one whose work is, shall we say, rather more in sympathy with my own ideas than those of Mr Charlesworth.'

This time everyone was too shocked to gasp, and no wonder. Miranda could hardly believe it herself. He had actually changed contractors! Ralph wouldn't like that. He wouldn't like it one bit, and, besides, who on earth had Ben found to take his place? Ralph was the largest and best-known local builder, and there were even occasionally rumours to the effect that he wasn't too fussy about how he dealt with any potential competition.

'But there isn't anyone else,' Bob was saying, certainly voicing all their thoughts.

'Not locally, perhaps,' Ben agreed. 'But if one looks hard enough one can generally find what one is seeking.'

He looked directly at Miranda when he spoke, and for some reason that look set off a chain of explosive physical reactions inside her body, making her long to be able to sit down so that he wouldn't be able to see that she was actually almost visibly trembling from the effect he was having on her.

'I contacted the Georgian Society,' he added by way of explanation, 'and they were able to put me in touch with a firm in Bath, who, as luck would have it, are just between contracts at the moment.

'I've been to see them, and it's arranged that they will take over the work with effect from tomorrow.'

There was a small silence while they all assimilated what he had said, and Miranda suspected that she wasn't the only one wondering how on earth Ralph had reacted to the news that he was being supplanted.

Ben remained for another half an hour, patiently going over the plans with them. Miranda deliberately kept herself in the background, but all the time she was acutely conscious of him; of the way he moved, of the way he spoke, but most of all of the way he would occasionally search the table, as though deliberately looking for her.

Which *must* be her imagination, because he could have no reason for wanting to seek her out, even if when he had walked in here earlier in the evening he had verbally implied that there was an intimacy between them... a relationship.

Which was all nonsense. She was letting her small-town upbringing blot out reality. Ben was a big-city man; in the city a man could claim the acquaintance of a woman without anyone else in earshot immediately assuming that he was romantically interested in her.

Not in this town he couldn't, though. By tomorrow it would be all over the place... a juicy item of gossip to be relished over morning coffee.

Quite deliberately, when Ben was taking his leave of the others Miranda escaped to the Ladies. She wasn't going to be singled out by him again and add even further fuel to the gossip.

As it was, when she returned she had to run the gauntlet of several curious and assessing looks, not to mention head off the questions of several of her co-committee members.

When the meeting broke up at half-past ten, she was tired enough to be glad she was going straight home.

As she edged her way through the now crowded bar, she heard Ralph Charlesworth's raised voice from one of the tables.

Ralph was a heavy drinker in addition to his other unpleasant traits. His voice sounded slurred and angry.

As Miranda headed for the door she heard him saying viciously, 'Well, if he thinks he can get away with this, I'll soon show him different,' and the shiver that struck her skin as she walked outside wasn't entirely due to the cool night air.

If, as she suspected, Ralph had been talking about Ben, then Ben had made a bad enemy. Ralph didn't play by the rules, and if Ben had dismissed him and got in fresh contractors... Her conscience urged her that someone would have to warn Ben that Ralph could be out to make trouble for him, but she couldn't face the thought of contacting him herself. Perhaps if she spoke with her father. She sighed faintly as she unlocked her car. It was unfortunate that Helen should be related to Ralph's wife, but then this was the sort of thing that happened in a small town, and Helen herself made no bones about her dislike of her relative by marriage.

Yes, in the morning she would have to have a word with her father. She ignored the small voice that warned her that she could save time and effort by getting in touch with Ben direct, thinking bitterly, So what if she was being a coward? Wasn't it better to be a coward than to risk the pain of...?

Of what? Of loving someone who didn't return that love?

*Loving* someone...

This was ridiculous, she told herself grimly as she drove home. As far as she was concerned, love and Ben Frobisher were two completely opposing forces.

But what if they weren't... what if they could be combined... what if...?

What if she stopped daydreaming and concentrated on reality for a change? she told herself sternly. What if she gave her time and attention not to daydreaming, but to working out how on earth she was going to find an effective counter to the rumours that would be running like summer weeds through the town by this time tomorrow?

It was too late now to regret her outspoken and oft-voiced views on the idiocy of falling in love, on the repressive state of marriage, at least where a woman was concerned, and her belief that a career and the independence that went with it were far more fulfilling than marriage and children.

All right, so maybe recently she *had* started to wonder if she hadn't perhaps been a little too vehement in her outspokenness... if she perhaps hadn't taken a long enough view and seen that maybe, just maybe, if a woman was determined and cool-headed enough, she could have it all—career, independence, marriage and children; but as yet this turn-around in her thinking was still her own secret.

The news that she was apparently involved with a man like Ben Frobisher was bound to provoke a good deal of light-hearted, and some not so light-hearted amusement at her expense. And of course once they had actually seen him, none of her friends was ever going to believe that she hadn't fallen head over heels in love with him.

Damn, damn, damn, she swore crossly. Why did he have to decide to move here and cause me all this trouble? Well, there was one thing he most definitely was not going to do and that was spoil a second night's sleep for her. Tonight there would be no dreams about intensely passionate kisses, no nocturnal yearnings for the kind of physical intimacy that surely belonged to one's teenage years, and not to the maturity of one's late twenties.

# CHAPTER FIVE

MIRANDA sighed as the telephone on her desk shrilled abruptly, breaking into her train of thought. She was still only halfway through the monthly piece on the housing market which she wrote for the local paper. Normally this was a task she thoroughly enjoyed, but today for some reason she was finding it difficult to focus her thoughts on her writing.

She reached for the receiver automatically, stifling her irritation when she heard the excited voice of one of her friends.

'Well, you are a dark horse, aren't you?' she was challenged. 'You never said a word to us about Ben Frobisher when you had dinner with John and me last week——'

'Because there wasn't anything to tell you, and there still isn't,' Miranda interrupted her firmly.

Obviously the town grapevine had got to work even more speedily than she had envisaged.

'Oh, come on. It's all over town, how he couldn't take his eyes off you at last night's meeting...'

'Rubbish,' Miranda told her curtly. 'I barely know the man.'

'You were with him at the golf club do,' her friend pointed out slyly. 'Or is that just a rumour, too?'

Miranda paused and then admitted wryly, 'No, but I was partnering him simply because he's a business associate. Nothing more.'

'Uh-huh, so that passionate clinch the two of you were seen in was just—er—a business discussion, was it?'

Miranda knew she was trapped. Jenny was a good friend whom she valued, but she wasn't very good at keeping secrets and if Miranda told her the real reason Ben had been kissing her . . . well, it was impossible, she just couldn't.

'You could have a June wedding,' Jenny was telling her excitedly. 'There's still time.'

'Jenny!' Miranda expostulated impatiently. 'Ben Frobisher and I barely know one another, and as for our getting married . . . well, that's impossible.'

'Really? Does *he* know that? From what I've heard, he sounds like one very determined man. A very dishy man as well, by all accounts. Look, why don't you bring him over to dinner one night? We'd love to meet him.'

Miranda groaned.

'Jenny for the last time, Ben Frobisher and I do not have the sort of relationship that extends to going out to dinner together.'

'Mm. Still at the stage when you prefer to be alone together, is that it? I remember when I first met John . . .'

Knowing how impossible it was to get her friend to change tack once she had set her mind in a certain groove, Miranda gave up. At least now Jenny had been distracted into talking about her own life, and as for the rumours and gossip which were obviously flying about the town . . . well, the proof of the pudding, as the saying went, was in the eating, and although she suspected she was going to be in for an uncomfortable month or so while everyone speculated on the outcome of her imagined relationship with Ben, once people realised that there simply was no relationship, the gossip would die down.

After she had replaced the receiver, she went out into the main office and asked Liz not to put any more calls through to her.

'I've got to finish this piece for the paper,' she told her with a groan, 'and at the moment I'm rather struggling with it.'

'Will do,' Liz assured her, adding, 'Oh, and by the way, your father said to tell you that he's taking the afternoon off.'

'Golfing, is he?' Miranda asked wryly.

Liz laughed. 'No, as a matter of fact he and Helen are going in to Bath. Helen said she was beginning to panic that she'd be walking down the aisle in the suit she wore for Linda Holmes's wedding last year unless she finds something soon.' They both laughed, and then Liz added, 'I'm going out for a sandwich soon. Want me to get you something?'

'Please. I doubt if I'm going to get much chance to get out of the office today. I've got reports to do on those two cottages I inspected last week.'

'No good?' Liz asked her sympathetically.

'Well, they're basically sound, but they need a lot of work doing on them, and I mean a lot of work, and the guy who's selling them doesn't seem to realise that at the moment we're in a buyers' market. The price he wants for them is far too high. Anyway, I'd better get back to my article.'

'Good luck, and don't worry. I'll field all your calls for you.'

An hour later, when Liz came in with the sandwich she had ordered and a mug of coffee, Miranda was astounded to discover that it was lunchtime.

Thanking the other woman, she pushed aside her notes and picked up the copy of *Country Life* which had been delivered with the morning papers.

As she scrutinised the houses advertised in it and ate her lunch, she deliberately refused to allow herself to dwell on her earlier telephone call or Ben Frobisher. Let the gossips embroider the facts as much as they wished. Sooner or later the truth would become obvious. Even so... She looked up from the magazine, and frowned. It would have helped if Ben himself hadn't played into their hands last night, and as for that kiss at the golf club being witnessed...

Don't think about that kiss, she advised herself hastily, almost choking as she gulped at her still too hot coffee.

It was gone two o'clock before she had finished her article to her satisfaction. It was her normal practice to walk round to the offices of the local paper with it, and it seemed silly to deviate from this habit simply because her route to the paper took her right past Ben's house in the High Street. As she pulled on her jacket, she asked herself scoffingly if she intended to spend the rest of her life

avoiding using one of the town's main thorough-
fares, simply because of the remote chance that she
might see Ben Frobisher.

He probably wouldn't even be there, she told
herself briskly, as she told Liz where she was going
and opened the office door.

It was a blustery March day, the wind soft and
warm with the promise of spring, and the clouds
high and white overhead in a vividly blue sky.

She didn't even manage to get across the town
square before she was stopped. Sighing, she smiled
a greeting at Lillian Forsyth, the wife of the vicar.

'I've been hearing the good news about last
night's committee meeting,' Lillian told her. 'I'm
sorry I missed it. It's wonderful news, though, isn't
it? I mean, to have someone new coming into the
town who's obviously as keen as us to preserve its
character. Bob was saying that he thought it might
be a good idea to invite him on to the committee.
As he pointed out, having such a successful
entrepreneur among our ranks is bound to add
weight to our cause. Actually I suspect he's
probably going to be in touch with you about it. I
get the impression that the general feeling is that
you be nominated to approach him to see how he
feels about joining us officially.'

'Me?' Miranda questioned, her heart sinking.

'Well, yes. In view of your...your friendship with
him.'

Her heart sank even further. Lillian Forsyth was
beginning to look slightly embarrassed. Miranda
knew she had caught the sharp edge in her voice,
and told herself that it was hardly the vicar's wife's

fault if her relationship with Frobisher had been exaggerated into something it was most definitely not.

'Well, I'll certainly ask my father to approach him if that's what the committee wants,' Miranda told her. 'He knows Ben—Mr Frobisher far better than I do. After all, he was the one who sold him the house and not me.'

If she had hoped by this statement to underline the fact that her acquaintance with Ben Frobisher was confined purely to business and existed only through her father, she soon realised that she had been over-optimistic, as Lillian Forsyth floundered and asked uncertainly, 'Oh, but I thought...that is... Well, I'd better get on. There's a WI meeting this evening.'

As she walked into the High Street, Miranda deliberately crossed over the road so that she was on the opposite side from the house Ben had bought, and as she drew level with it she deliberately increased her pace and avoided looking at it.

And yet traitorously her heart started to thump far more heavily than her brisk walking pace necessitated, and there was an unfamiliar tight sensation of apprehension-cum-excitement constricting her chest.

When she was several yards past the house she slackened her pace, crossly refusing to acknowledge that the feeling she was experiencing owed more to disappointment than relief.

To punish herself for this emotional treachery to her own best interests, once she had delivered her piece to the newspaper editor, she deliberately took a circuitous route back to the office.

'Any calls?' she asked Liz when she opened the door.

'Only one ... from Ben Frobisher,' Liz told her, studiously keeping her voice blank of all expression. 'I told him you weren't available, so he said to tell you that he'd pick you up here at five-thirty.'

'He'd *what*?' Miranda could scarcely believe what she had just heard.

'He said to tell you he'd pick you up at five-thirty. Something about showing you the plans for the conversion. He said you hadn't had an opportunity to see them with the others last night. He said you'd know all about it and be expecting his call.'

'Did he leave a number?' Miranda asked her dangerously. She was seething with anger. What on earth did he think he was doing? Wasn't it enough that he had already stirred up all sorts of gossip about the pair of them, without adding this? But at least only Liz had heard him on this occasion. She worried at her bottom lip, and then asked unevenly, 'Liz, would you mind ... could I ask you?'

The other girl waited, watching her a little uncertainly.

'I ... that is, my relationship with Ben Frobisher ... I'd rather no one else knew about his phone call,' she told her uncomfortably. 'If you wouldn't mind keeping it to yourself.'

Immediately Liz's face fell.

'Oh, I'm sorry, Miranda,' she apologised. 'Obviously I wouldn't tell a soul, but unfortunately Anne Soames was in here when he rang ... and Mr

Frobisher does have very good diction. You know what she's like... I'm afraid she must have heard virtually the whole conversation.'

Miranda's heart sank.

Anne Soames was one of the worst gossips in the area. Never maliciously so, and certain allowances had to be made for her as since she had been widowed three years earlier she had been very lonely, but, of all the people to have overheard Ben's telephone call, she was the one Miranda would have most wanted not to have done so.

'Look, I am sorry,' Liz told her gently. 'And I do understand what it's like when you first start a new relationship. You want to keep it to yourself... especially——'

Miranda suppressed a strong desire to scream and gritted her teeth to say bitterly, 'On, no, Liz, not you as well! Look, there *is* no relationship between Ben Frobisher and me, other than that he was a client of this firm, and as one of its partners I accompanied him to last week's golf club do to make up the numbers. As for all this extraordinary gossip that's flying around... Why on earth can't people learn to mind their own business?' She stopped, aware that she was probably a little unfair. 'I'm sorry,' she apologised, 'but there are times when living in a small town surrounded by people who've known you all your life can be very...

'Ben Frobisher is an acquaintance, nothing more. Can you imagine how I'm going to feel when all this gossip reaches his ears, as it must?'

'Perhaps if you explained to him,' Liz suggested.

'Explained what? That half the town has got the two of us paired up together and married off on the strength of last week's golf club do, an unwise comment he made at last night's committee meeting, and one telephone call? He'll think me certifiable. He's a Londoner. He won't understand. He'll think——'

She stopped abruptly. What was it she was afraid of him thinking? That she was trying to force some kind of intimacy between them by fostering the gossip, by allowing it to run unchecked? But the gossip wasn't *her* fault. *She* wasn't the one who had singled him out at last night's meeting... She wasn't the one who had telephoned him ... she wasn't ...

Oh, what was the use? Oh, what was the use in allowing herself to get all worked up about something over which she had absolutely no control? she reflected wearily; but as for tonight ... well, she would soon make it plain to Ben that she wasn't remotely interested in seeing his precious plans and that she certainly did not welcome the kind of high-handed attitude he had engaged in today, ringing up like that and behaving as though he had every right to claim her time. It would serve him right if she decided to leave the office early and go straight home. But she knew she would not do that. For one thing they didn't normally close until five-thirty, and in her father's absence she would have to remain here until that time.

When Liz left at four-thirty for a dental appointment, Miranda struggled with a wilful impulse to close down the office early. In the end her conscience and training won, and she realised that she would have to stay until five-thirty.

However, what she could do was to make sure that she was ready to leave at five-thirty on the dot so that if Ben Frobisher was even a couple of minutes late he would have missed her.

As luck would have it, at twenty past five, just as she was getting ready to leave, the phone rang, and she was still dealing with the call when Ben walked into the office at five-thirty sharp.

When he saw that she was busy, he went and sat down discreetly out of earshot, picking up a magazine and studying it with apparent interest while she dealt with the caller's query.

He wasn't, she noticed darkly, carrying anything with him, and there was certainly no room in the soft leather blouson jacket he was wearing for him to conceal the large set of plans she had seen the previous night.

'I'm sorry about that,' she apologised in a clipped voice as she replaced the receiver. It was good manners rather than genuine regret that made her apologise. In point of fact, she had been uncomfortably conscious as she'd replaced the receiver that the plastic had become rather damp where she had been holding it and that her fingers were stiff and tense. Why did he have to have this effect on her? she wondered bitterly as she kept her distance from him.

He had got to his feet as she replaced the receiver, and now he was walking towards her. Why was it that she was so aware of him, so conscious of his maleness, of his sexuality? She licked her lips nervously as she realised that she had been wondering what he would look like without his jacket and the shirt he was wearing beneath it, whether in fact his torso would be as firmly fleshed and tautly muscled as his lithe movements suggested, whether the thick dark hair on his head was mirrored on his body, and if so what it would be like to trace its path with her fingertips and with her lips.

Aghast at the direction of her own thoughts, she turned her back on him and demanded shakily, 'The plans . . . Liz said you wanted to show them to me.'

'Yes, I do,' he agreed. 'I don't have them with me, though. They are over at my place. I thought perhaps we could have dinner together, go over the plans and then I could pick your brains a little. I still haven't found somewhere permanent to live and your father intimated to me that you're the expert on your more outlying properties.'

Her father. Miranda ground her teeth. Why on earth had she *ever* agreed to her father's request that she partner Ben at the golf club dance?

She opened her mouth to tell him that it was impossible for her to have dinner with him, and that she had no desire whatsoever to see his plans, but just as she did so a movement outside in the square caught her eye, and as she focused on it she saw that Ralph Charlesworth was walking determinedly towards the office.

Her heart sank. This wouldn't be the first time that Ralph had used the excuse of wanting to discuss the purchase of a property with her to force her to endure his company. As a building contractor, he did occasionally buy property on a speculative basis, and she had felt obliged to deal as professionally with his spurious interest as she could, while ignoring the sexual innuendo of his conversation. Behind her she could hear Ben asking calmly, 'Are you ready to leave or...?'

'Yes. Yes, I'm ready,' she told him quickly, grabbing her coat and bag. Much as her brain warned her that it was not in her own best interest for her to spend any time at all in Ben Frobisher's company and risk exposing herself to the emotional and physical impact he seemed to have on her, when it came to a choice between Ben and Ralph...

She gave a small shudder, as Ben opened the door for her and then waited while she locked it behind her.

As she fell into step beside Ben, she was acutely conscious of Ralph's silent presence behind them, watching them.

She had assumed that Ben hadn't seen Ralph, but as they crossed the square she realised she was wrong because he said quietly to her, 'Charlesworth hasn't been bothering you again, has he?'

She shook her head, and then remembered something she had forgotten in the busyness of the day. 'I don't think he's very pleased about losing the contract for your conversion.'

'He told you that, did he?' Ben queried, his voice suddenly a little harder than it had been.

Whether by accident of design, Miranda didn't know, but his car was parked next to her own, and as she removed her car keys from her handbag she told him truthfully, 'No. I just happened to overhear him saying something to somebody else as I left the meeting last night. He was in the bar; he'd obviously been drinking. He wasn't making any effort to keep his voice down and, while he didn't specifically mention your name, I had the feeling from the threats I overheard that he was determined to pay you out for taking him off the contract. I could be wrong.'

'Mm. Well, maybe . . . maybe not. As it happens, on the advice of the new contractors I have already organised for the house to be guarded at night when it's empty. Apparently it isn't uncommon in and around Bath for houses under conversion and empty to be stripped of their period detailings. There's a thriving market in reclaimed authentic period fittings.

'You know the place I'm renting?' he queried as he turned to unlock his own car door.

Miranda nodded her head, and realised too late as he opened his car door and got inside that it was impossible now for her to tell him that she had changed her mind and didn't want to see the plans.

The cottage he was renting was on the opposite side of the town from her own, but just as remote.

As she followed Ben's car down the lane which led to it, she reflected that its vaguely shabby exterior betrayed the fact that it lacked a loving permanent inhabitant, and, once she had parked her car next to Ben's and followed him inside, this impression was borne out by the appearance of the kitchen.

Like her own, it was a comfortably sized rectangular room, and also like her own it was warmed by a large Aga set in what must have been the original chimney breast, but there the similarities ended.

While her own kitchen had been lovingly planned to complement the building's ancient beams and low ceilings, this room had suffered the careless modernisation of an owner more intent on turning it into something that was strictly functional, rather than sympathetically taking into account the age and character of the building.

Stark white kitchen units, more suited to a modern streamlined flat, had been installed along two walls, and in the centre of the room, where Miranda had the heavy old scrubbed oak table she had lovingly rescued from a local sale-room, there was a glaringly out-of-place chrome and glass table and four equally unsuitable chairs.

Ben must have seen the expression on her face because he grimaced a little and agreed, 'Not exactly in character, is it?'

'Not really.'

'Fortunately the sitting-room's rather more pleasant and luckily there's a good-sized table in there so that we can eat——'

He stopped as Miranda made a small sound in her throat.

'Something wrong?' he asked her.

'I ... well ... when you said we'd have dinner, I assumed you meant that we'd be eating out,' she was forced to admit.

The grin he gave her was almost boyish.

'Ah, I see, you don't trust my cooking, is that it? Well, you needn't worry. Ma made a point of ensuring that we could all cook. Not that I'm any expert.'

Miranda swallowed hard, unwilling to admit that it wasn't so much his cooking she feared as the thought of being totally alone with him, and even then it was not him she feared, but herself, or rather her reaction to him.

Despairingly she wished that she had stood by her initial decision to tell him that she was too busy to see the plans, but it was too late for that now.

'What do you want to do? See the plans first and then eat, or...?'

She thought frantically and then realised that if she looked at the plans first she would be able to tell him that she didn't have time to stay for dinner and would be able to leave.

'Er—the plans first, I think.'

She cursed inwardly, wishing she could make her voice sound more forceful, more professional. As it was, it had all the uncertain, husky resonance of an adolescent trying not to betray herself to the object of her adoring crush.

She really had to pull herself together, she told herself severely, and yet, despite the fact that the kitchen was a good size and that they were virtually separated by the full width of it, she was still acutely conscious of Ben as a man.

'Right, then,' he agreed cheerfully. 'The plans it is.'

The sitting-room was, as he had said, far less aggressively modernised than the kitchen, but it was also rather over-full of furniture, which meant that, once he had unrolled the plans and spread them on the table, in order to be able to see them Miranda had to stand so close to him that their bodies were practically touching.

Thank goodness the town gossips could not see them now, she reflected idly as Ben leaned forward and started to point out details of the plan to her.

'And you can see how we intend to retain all the existing period features,' he was saying to her.

Unwisely she made the mistake of turning her head to look at him. Unlike most men she knew, he didn't seem to favour the use of cologne or aftershave, but there was still a clean tangy scent clinging to his skin, a potent male scent that made her feel faintly dizzy and light-headed. Her gaze slid helplessly to his mouth. He was still speaking to her, but she no longer heard the words. Her heart had started to beat far too fast as she remembered her dream and how he had kissed her.

Her mouth had gone very dry, her body felt hot, her skin somehow extra sensitive, so that when he breathed out and she felt the warmth of that exhaled breath it immediately raised a rash of goosepimples against her flesh and made her shudder slightly as the sensation of his breath against her skin set off a chain of lightning reaction throughout her body.

When she felt her nipples actually stiffen and start to swell, she was so shocked that she actually started to glance down at her own flesh, as though unable to believe the message it was giving her.

To her chagrin she could see quite clearly against the crisp outline of her shirt the unmistakable arousal of her body, and dark flags of mortification flamed in her face as she stood there praying that Ben hadn't noticed and wishing there was some way she could turn her back on him.

When she heard him saying, 'It's rather cold in here. I ought to have lit the fire,' her embarrassment increased. Did he *really* think she was cold, or was he just trying to be polite? Or had he, please God, not even noticed the betraying evidence of those twin flaunting witnesses to her physical awareness of him? If only she hadn't left her jacket in her car... but it was too late to regret that now; the only thing she could do was to pick up the cue he had given her and agree unevenly that, yes, it was rather chilly.

'If you can hold on for a couple of minutes I'll get the fire going. It is laid,' he told her, smiling at her.

In other circumstances she would have been grateful to him for his circumspection and for the tactful way he avoided even giving the briefest glance in the direction of her body, but, as it was, all his tact did was to increase her own feeling of humiliation. It was all her own fault. If she hadn't started thinking about that damned dream.

Miserably she pretended to be studying the plans while Ben crossed over to the fire. He had removed his jacket when they came inside, and now, out of the corner of her eye, she was aware of him rolling up the sleeves of his shirt. His forearms were tautly muscled, the skin smooth and firm.

An odd yearning, yielding sensation started to spread through her body, making her feel weak and shaky. As Ben put a match to the ready-laid fire, the flames flared up, their light glinting on the dark hairs coating his arms.

His arms . . . Her heart was pounding frantically, she discovered, a feverish flush of heat burning her skin. She suffered an almost uncontrollable desire to walk over to him and to touch his hard flesh. His skin would feel warm, not clammily so, but with the texture of expensive satin. The dark hairs would be crisp beneath her sensitive fingertips, and when she touched her lips to the inner curve of his elbow his whole body would tense in response to her caress. He would reach for her then, holding her so that they were kneeling body to body, and he would kiss her as he had done in her dream, sliding his hand into her hair, his fingers trembling silently against her scalp, his mouth gentle at first and then hungry—demanding. And as he kissed her he would draw her closer to him, so close that her breasts were pressed flat against his chest, the stimulation of his body moving against her own, causing her nipples to stiffen and ache.

He would kiss her jaw and her throat, sliding away her shirt, unfastening its buttons until he had revealed the soft curves of her breasts. He would gaze at her then, his breath caught in his throat, his hands tender as they touched her body. He would bend his head and slowly caress her naked breasts and when he did she would bury her fingers in his hair, holding him prisoner against her as she arched her body in flagrant enticement.

'Are you all right?'

The question cut across her thoughts, wrenching her back to reality. She could feel her face burning as she tried to focus on what he was saying. She had been so lost in her thoughts, in her fantasy, that she hadn't even realised he had moved away from the fire and was coming towards her; instinctively she bent her head over the plans, letting her hair swing forward, hoping, praying that what she had been thinking hadn't been visible in her expression.

'I'm fine,' she managed to tell him huskily as he joined her at the table.

'Well, the room should warm up pretty soon now,' he told her, and went on, 'The architect believes that originally the staircase would have been open to the roof, not sealed off on each floor as it is now. The new contractors agree with him, and they've suggested doing some investigative work to see if he's correct. If so, it might be worthwhile trying to restore the staircase to what it was originally. Look, here's their sketch for how the house would look if we reverted to that plan.'

Miranda focused desperately on the plans. Her mind and body were in total chaos. She felt as though she were undergoing some kind of breakdown, she reflected dazedly as she tried to focus on where Ben was indicating. She couldn't believe what was happening to her; that she had actually stood there and imagined... Her mouth had gone dry again and her heart was pounding.

'No, you're looking in the wrong place,' Ben was saying to her. 'Perhaps if I stand here.'

To her consternation, she felt him move behind her and come to stand so close to her that she could feel the warmth coming off his body, and knew without turning round that all she had to do was to move an inch or so to come into physical contact with him. He stretched out his left arm as he leaned forward, placing his hand flat on the desk so that she was virtually imprisoned by his body. 'Look, here is the sketch,' he was saying to her, indicating with his right hand where she was to look.

Hesitantly she did so. She felt almost sick with tension and shock. She had never once in her life envisaged that she could ever feel like this...react like this. To imagine such intimacies with a man she barely knew...to want such intimacies to the extent...

She flicked her tongue nervously against her dry lips.

Against her ear, she heard Ben saying teasingly, 'It might help if we tucked this out of the way, so,' and unbelievably his hand stroked through the fine softness of her hair, tucking it behind her ear.

It was something she herself did a hundred times a day, a gesture so automatic and taken for granted that, if anyone had ever told her that to have it performed by someone else would prove so sensual and disturbing an experience that she would literally be shaking with the effort of controlling her reaction, she would have laughed at them, or accused them of indulging in a bout of over-imagination. But she would have been wrong. Just that light brush of Ben's fingers against her skin, a movement so casual, so clinical almost, so devoid of anything even remotely lover-like, had still been enough to set off such an explosive chain of sensation within her body that she felt physically exhausted by the intensity of them.

She couldn't endure any more. If she had to stay here much longer...

'The plans are marvellous, Ben,' she started to gabble. 'I take back everything I said. I'm afraid I really must leave, though.'

'Leave? But what about dinner?'

Dinner. Dinner? Did he honestly expect her to sit down and calmly pretend... She gave a small shudder, and fibbed frantically, 'I'm sorry. I'd forgotten, but I've already arranged to see an old friend this evening. Her husband's away on business and she's all on her own. It had completely slipped my mind until you were showing me the plans.'

'I see.'

She suspected that he didn't believe her. There was a coldness in his eyes and his voice as he stepped back from her that warned her that he had probably guessed she was lying. But just so long as he hadn't guessed *why* she was lying.

He insisted on accompanying her to her car and, opening the door for her as she got in, he leaned down towards her and said, 'Thanks once again for warning me about Charlesworth.'

'One good turn deserves another,' Miranda quipped shakily. 'After all, you did save me from him at the golf club do.'

'Mm, I did, didn't I?'

He was, she realised, looking at her mouth, causing a nervous fluttery sensation to run riot through her body.

'I'm sorry you can't stay for dinner. Still, if you have a prior engagement...'

'A prior engagement,' she repeated stupidly, unable to drag her gaze from his, unable to forget the way he had looked at her mouth and made her feel as though...as though he wanted to kiss it.

'Yes...with your friend. The one whose husband is away.'

The iron was back in his voice, the coolness in his eyes.

She tried to start the car, but her fingers were trembling so much she couldn't turn the key properly until the third attempt.

'Drive carefully,' he told her as she finally got the engine started.

Drive carefully... Only when she was sure that he wouldn't be standing there watching her any longer did she allow herself to look into her rear-view mirror. What would have happened if she had told him the truth...that there was no friend...that she had lied in a desperate attempt to get away from him because...because...she couldn't trust herself to be with him and not betray what she was feeling? When he had looked at her mouth just then, it had been almost as though he was willing her to do something. Like what? Invite him to kiss her?

She shuddered wildly, her hands sticky with perspiration as she clung to the steering-wheel. She was letting her imagination create fantasies that had no place in reality, imposing her own feelings, her own desires on to him. Horror-struck, she tried to control her careering thoughts. What was happening to her? Less than a week ago she had been a completely normal, sane, level-headed twenty-eight-year-old. Now... now she was heading with all the folly, all the idiocy, all the illogicality of a woman who had fallen instantly and hopelessly in love.

In love. 'Please, God, no,' she whispered through gritted teeth. Bad enough that she should desire him, but to love him as well...!

## CHAPTER SIX

THAT night Miranda had the dream again, only this time it was stronger, clearer. She woke up with her body wet with sweat and her heart pounding, an ache in the pit of her stomach that made her go scarlet with embarrassment and guilt, even though there was no one there to witness her confusion.

How *could* she have dreamed like that, experiencing sensations and needs she had never even known? Her fingertips still burned as though they had actually come into contact with Ben's flesh, her lips actually stung as though they had truly been kissed with all the force and desire Ben had evidenced in her dream.

How could a dream be so real, so physical? she asked herself sickly as she got out of bed. Her throat felt dry, and her body ached. What she needed was a calming drink of herbal tea. Something to soothe her over-inflamed nerves and send her back to sleep—a dreamless sleep this time.

Even now, when she was fully awake, she still couldn't banish the memory of her dream intimacy with Ben. How had it happened? How had her mind, her subconscious been able to furnish her with such a shockingly intimate mental image of his body, of his touch, with so strong and lingering a sensation of having been held in his arms, of having been caressed . . . loved by him?

As her conscious mind flinched from the memories she was trying to suppress, the cup she was holding slipped from her fingers, smashing on the kitchen's stone-flagged floor with a noise that hurt her eardrums. As she bent down to pick up the broken shards of pottery, one stabbed sharply into her finger.

A few minutes later, sucking it where it was still bleeding, she stared broodingly out through the window into the darkness.

This idiocy had to stop. It was almost unbelievable that she, who had prided herself on being so in control of her life, should now feel as though that control had been wrested from her; that her life was in fact frighteningly out of control.

If she could just find a way to stop having these dreams. She shivered as she sipped the herbal tea she had brewed, wrapping her fingers round the cup, and trying to force her thoughts into some kind of order.

There *must* be a way she could get back in control of her life...of her emotions...of her needs. All right, so she found Ben Frobisher physically desirable—there was no point in trying to deny that, at least not to herself—but that did not mean that he had to invade her dreams every night, taking over her subconscious, revealing to her needs...emotions...feelings she had never hitherto experienced.

She padded restlessly around her kitchen, telling herself fiercely that it was useless trying to blame Ben for her dreams; that the fault, the guilt, the blame lay with her.

But what if it wasn't merely physical desire she felt for him...what if it was something else...something stronger...deeper...and far, far more dangerous? What if...what if what? What if she loved him?

She tried to deny the thought as she had tried to deny it before, but it remained lodged in her consciousness, refusing to go away, no matter how much she tried to evade or bury it.

Tonight at his cottage she had felt so...so frightened and helpless...so caught up in what she was feeling that she had had no control left to fight it; and even after she had left him, even after she had driven safely away, she had still ached for him, had still wanted to turn her car round and go back, to tell him she had changed her mind, to beg him to allow her to stay with him.

She shivered, putting down her empty cup. If she didn't go back to bed soon, she might as well not bother. Already her disturbed nights were beginning to tell on her. She must stop thinking about him, she told herself wearily as she went back upstairs. She must find a way of blotting him out of her thoughts...out of her dreams.

Easy to say, but far, far harder to do, she acknowledged tiredly half an hour later, lying rigidly awake in her bed, too afraid to allow her tired body to relax into the sleep it needed.

A week passed without her seeing Ben. A casual remark by her father informed her that he was apparently in London working and wouldn't be returning until the following week.

Ironically, when this information should have relaxed her, all it actually did was to increase her tension, to make her even more fearful of allowing him to slide into her thoughts in her unguarded moments.

Every day she told herself that today she would not think about him, and yet every day, somehow or other, she would find that treacherously she was doing exactly that.

She even went out and bought herself a child's money-box, which she kept on her desk and into which she made herself pay a small monetary fine whenever her determination not to think about him lapsed.

When, after only three days, she had virtually filled the money-box, she was forced to admit that by providing it in the first place she had been subconsciously encouraging her own self-betrayal.

As another measure to keep him out of her thoughts she resolved to avoid going anywhere near the house in the High Street, and yet every day or so, it seemed, she managed to find an equally valid and important reason why she should break this decision.

She attended the monthly meeting of another of her committees, and gritted her teeth when she was gently quizzed by some of its older members about her new 'boyfriend'.

Even her father had heard the gossip, and had looked mildly surprised when she had rounded on him quite fiercely when he'd asked her if it was true that she and Ben were going together.

'No, we are not,' she had told him bitingly, adding, 'Honestly, Dad, you know what this place is like for gossip.'

'Sorry,' he apologised. 'Pity, though. Nice chap. Helen's invited him to the wedding, by the way.'

The wedding was only ten days away. Helen had found the perfect outfit in Bath, reminding Miranda that she had still to find something suitable to wear.

Pointing out to her father that she would be in sole charge of the agency while he was enjoying his leisurely honeymoon, she claimed the privilege of daughter as well as partner and told him that she intended to take a day off in order to go out and buy herself a new outfit.

Although he grumbled about it, Miranda knew him well enough to know that he didn't really mind.

She chose a Wednesday, their local half-day, which meant that the town and business would be relatively quiet.

It was some months since she had last visited Bath—prior to Christmas, in fact, in order to do her Christmas shopping—and, as always, she immediately fell under the city's architectural spell.

No, she didn't have anything specific in mind, she told the girl in the dress shop where she bought most of her clothes. A suit or separates, something smart, but perhaps not quite as businesslike as her normal choice of outfit.

'I think we've got just the thing,' the girl told her, smiling. 'A range of separates made in Germany. Pricey, but very, very well-made.'

When she showed Miranda the rail of separates she had in mind, Miranda had to admit that the clothes were beautifully made, and highly desirable. They were also, as she had said, expensive.

'Look, why don't you try this on?' the girl suggested, producing a two-piece suit in cool cream wool. The jacket was long-sleeved with a slightly scooped neckline. It fastened with a double row of buttons and should really, the girl told her, be worn buttoned up without a shirt beneath it. The skirt that went with it was plain and straight, and the jacket was adorned with a variety of gold-coloured letters in metal.

'It's very different,' the girl told her, 'very simple and smart, and yet at the same time rather eye-catching.'

'Very,' Miranda agreed, eyeing the suit uncertainly. It was rather more high-profile than she had had in mind.

'Try it on,' the girl suggested again. 'If you don't like it, I'm sure we can soon find something else.'

Uncertainly Miranda did so.

The suit fitted perfectly, and as she stepped out of the cubicle and caught sight of her reflection in the mirrors she tensed in surprise.

'It looks very good on you,' the girl told her easily. 'But if you don't feel comfortable in it ... I know it's rather different from your normal taste, but you did say ... I don't want to pressure you into having something you won't enjoy wearing.'

Miranda gave a rueful smile. The suit might have been made for her, and, if the truth were known, once she had got over the shock of seeing her own reflection she had been forced to admit that the suit did look good on her.

'It's not going to be something I can wear too often,' she murmured.

'You mean people aren't going to forget it!' the girl laughed. 'Well, if you like, after the wedding we could probably remove the gold letters which will make it rather less striking, and if you want to get rather more mileage out of it, well, I can show you some other things from the same range which will go with it.'

In the end, Miranda couldn't resist not only buying the suit, but in addition a smart bright red light wool jacket to wear over the cream skirt, another skirt in black, a silk shirt embroidered with bright red metallic and gilt hearts, and then, as a final act of defiant extravagance, a large cotton sweater and matching knitted jacket from the same range with American baseball motifs embroidered in gold, red and black on a background of the same cream as her original suit.

She blenched a little as she paid the bill, but reminded herself that it was quite a long time since she had been so self-indulgent.

It was only when she had left the shop and was looking for somewhere to have her lunch before looking for suitable shoes and a bag to go with her outfit that she acknowledged to herself that, while she had been trying on her new clothes, it hadn't been so much their usefulness for her lifestyle that had motivated her but the thought of Ben Frobisher's seeing her wearing them.

She stopped in mid-stride, frowning crossly. She had thought she had left behind her the totally idiotic urge to dress to impress the male sex, or rather a specific member of it, when she left her teens.

Thoroughly disgusted with herself, she paused, half tempted to go back to the shop and say she had changed her mind.

Sighing faintly to herself, she told herself that she was being utterly and completely ridiculous. She had bought the clothes and she was just going to have to live with that fact.

As she hurried into a small Italian restaurant, which was one of her favourites, she wondered a little wryly to herself how her father was going to react to her turning up for work wearing the very striking knitted sweater and jacket with its baseball motifs.

She didn't linger over her lunch. There were still shoes and a bag to buy, although that shouldn't take long; she had discovered years ago that the most comfortable court shoes for her feet were a very plain style by Charles Jourdan which, despite their heels, could be worn all day long without causing either her feet or her legs to ache; she also had to find a hat.

Their town was such that no one would ever dream of turning up for a wedding bareheaded. Even the bystanders, who gathered outside the church to watch the bride and groom emerging, were invariably dressed in their best, their heads sporting their 'wedding hats', and, little as she relished the idea, as the bridegroom's daughter she would be expected to wear a hat with a capital 'H'.

In the end, she found one in a small shop hidden down a side-street. Made of closely woven shiny black straw, it went perfectly with her suit, although when she saw the Frederick Fox label inside it her heart sank a little.

On her return journey to her car she happened to pass a bookshop with a window-display of the latest bestseller by one of her father's favourite crime writers. On impulse she went inside to buy it for him.

There was a long queue for the till, and apparently some kind of problem with the equipment, since two girls were trying to change the roll of paper inside it and apparently not succeeding. As she waited Miranda glanced absently at the books to the side of her. A title suddenly glared out at her: *'Your Dreams. Their Meaning and Interpretation.'*

Almost before she had realised what she was doing, she had reached for the book. She wasn't going to buy it, of course. Such stuff was all nonsense. She would just look at it . . . flip through it while she waited for the queue to move. But, before she had barely opened the book, the fault with the cash register was rectified and the queue started moving so rapidly that, when she moved forward, Miranda discovered she was still clutching it.

There was nothing else for it now. She would have to buy it. Self-consciously she presented it to the cashier with her other purchase, but the girl was totally uninterested in what she was buying, being intent on dealing with the long queue.

Once outside the shop, Miranda wondered why on earth she hadn't simply taken the book back and replaced it on the shelf. All right, so she would have lost her place in the queue...but so what?

Well, it was too late now. Just as well it hadn't been very expensive.

On her way home she detoured to call on Helen and show her her wedding outfit.

'It's fabulous,' Helen approved. 'And so nice to see you buying something young and flirty.'

'Flirty?' Miranda stared at her.

'Well, not flirty exactly,' Helen corrected herself. 'More...more...'

'Eye-catching,' Miranda supplied drily for her.

'Yes. That's it...eye-catching. By the way, has your father mentioned to you that we've invited Ben Frobisher to the wedding?'

'Yes, he has,' Miranda told her repressively, adding firmly, 'Helen, all this gossip that's been going around about the two of us is just that, you know—gossip.'

'Well, yes. *I* know that. But...well, at the golf club do I couldn't help noticing how interested he was in you.'

Ben, interested in her? Helen was letting her imagination and her own romance with her father go to her head.

'I don't think so,' she told Helen dismissively. 'It was business, that's all.'

'Really?'

The look Helen gave her made Miranda wonder a little uncomfortably if Helen too had heard about that kiss, and if so...

'I really must be going,' she told her hastily, scooping up her purchases and heading for the door.

She spent what was left of the daylight working in her garden, happily digging and weeding as she marvelled at the perseverance and strength of nature, crooning away contentedly to herself as she recognised, among the growing perennials in her border, familiar old friends.

The delphiniums she had bought and so carefully nurtured all through the previous summer, protecting them from the attentions of the voracious slugs which seemed to inhabit her border, were making good strong plants, repaying her care and attention with their new growth, and there were the granny's bonnets, just a froth of blue-green leaves at the moment, but later in the year their impossibly fine stems would carry the delicate nodding heads of the pretty trumpet-shaped blue and pink flowers.

When it started to grow dusky, she realised she had stayed out far later than she had intended. She was grubby and tired, and no doubt by tomorrow her back would be aching, but right now she felt more relaxed and in harmony with herself than she had in a long time.

She was still humming under her breath when she kicked off her wellingtons and walked into the kitchen. On the table in front of her was the book she had bought.

She tensed and stared at it, all the joy and peace draining out of her.

If she had any sense she would throw it away
right now. But for some reason she didn't. Instead,
she skirted the table as though the book were about
to pounce on her and hurried upstairs to shower
and get changed.

She would make herself a light meal, and then
she would settle down for a nice relaxing evening.
An evening which she was not going to allow to be
invaded by any disruptive thoughts about Ben
Frobisher.

With this thought in mind after her shower, she
changed into a soft loose top and an old pair of
jeans and went downstairs to make herself a meal.

While she ate it she studied one of her gardening
books, and as always was both depressed and
uplifted by the photographs in it of wonderfully
perfect gardens, where design and nature flowed
harmoniously into one another.

She was just wondering if she could perhaps have
a pergola running the width of her garden, dividing
it into two and providing a luscious, rose-scented
bower for her to enjoy during the summer months,
when someone knocked on her door.

Frowning, she went to see who it was, glancing
at the clock as she did so. It was just gone ten;
rather late for visitors.

Keeping the safety-chain fastened, she opened the
door and then froze as she saw Ben Frobisher
standing outside, his face illuminated in the light
from the doorway. He looked, she noticed
anxiously, as though he had been involved in some
kind of minor accident or a fight.

'Ben! What...?'

'I'm sorry, did I startle you?' he apologised as he saw the shock in her eyes.

She had automatically started to open the door properly, and as he stepped inside he told her, 'I had to call round, if only to thank you for your timely warning.'

'My warning? What warning?'

'About Charlesworth,' Ben reminded her as she closed the door behind him.

There was a rip in the sleeve of his jacket, she noticed, the kind that looked as though it might have been caused by a sharp object, such as a knife. She shivered sickly.

'I've been in London for the last few days,' Ben was telling her. 'I only got back late this afternoon. I went home and then I decided to go round and see how they were getting on with the conversion. Just as well I did,' he added grimly. 'I'd barely arrived there. In fact, I was upstairs checking something when four youths broke in through the back door. I heard the noise they were making, and rushed downstairs to find one of them about to hit Rob James, the security watchman, with a heavy piece of wood. When they realised he wasn't there on his own, I think it put the wind up them a bit. Two of them ran off straight away. The others...' His mouth compressed. 'One of them had a knife, the other... Well, there was a bit of a struggle, and unfortunately both of them got away. There was nothing to indicate that Charlesworth was responsible, of course, but in view of what you overheard...'

Miranda shivered. She *had* heard stories...rumours...vague whispers that one of the reasons Ralph had become so successful so quickly was because of his way of getting rid of any competition by using threatening tactics of violence or damage to property and possessions. As far as she knew, no one had ever been able to prove anything against him, but that did not stop the rumours from circulating.

'Did you call in the police?' she asked him.

'Yes, but, as they told us, there is really very little they could do. What *I* have done is arrange to get in another night watchman and to make sure that all the doors have proper security-locks on them.

'It makes my blood run cold to think what might have happened if I hadn't been there. One man against the four of them wouldn't have stood a chance.'

'No,' Miranda agreed gravely. She was still feeling slightly sick inside as she realised how easily Ben could have been hurt...or worse.

'I'm sorry,' Ben commented. 'I shouldn't have come barging in here like this, but I suppose I'm still so hyped up over the whole thing that I needed to talk it over with someone, and since *you* were the person to warn me about Charlesworth in the first place...'

'Let's go into the kitchen,' Miranda suggested. Tiny vibrations of shock were convulsing her body. 'I'll make us both a drink.' As he followed her into the kitchen an unpleasant thought struck her.

Could it be partially *her* fault that Ralph was trying to get at Ben, and not solely because he had lost the contract?

Ben was right behind her as she walked into the kitchen. She turned round immediately to ask him if she was in any way to blame, but the impulsive words were never spoken as the bright light of the kitchen revealed to her the blood drying on the cut on his face.

Without even thinking about what she was doing, she reached out instinctively to touch it, her eyes huge with pain and anxiety as her fingers trembled against it.

'You're hurt.'

The words trembled in the silence between them.

'Not really; it's just a scratch.' Ben's voice was equally strained, unsteady, his speech slow and almost slurred.

She wasn't sure how it had happened, but suddenly she was standing so close to him that she could feel the too-rapid thud of his heart, feel the heat coming off his skin.

'Miranda.'

As he whispered her name, drawing out every syllable, his arms came round her. It was like coming home, like finding peace. It was... it was like knowing that she had found a haven she had wanted all her life.

'He might have killed you.'

The words hurt her throat. She knew that she was trembling violently, that her eyes, her voice, must be betraying her to him, but she couldn't check the emotions filling her.

'No.'

The denial was soft but firm. He lifted her hand from his face and carried it to his lips gently kissing her palm, making her tremble again, but not this time with fear.

'Miranda...'

His hands were framing her face, his thumbs making gentle circular caresses against her skin. One of them touched her mouth, rubbing against her lower lip. He was looking right down into her eyes, and she could see the heat that burned in his, knew with a savage kick of sharp awareness that he wanted her, that in his heightened emotional state his adrenalin-fuelled anger had given way to physical desire.

As his thumb slowly caressed her bottom lip he bent his head towards her. She closed her eyes, clinging dizzily to him, shuddering beneath the force of the sensations engulfing her as his tongue touched the moist softness of her mouth.

Held in his arms, tightening around her, she felt his muscles contract; felt the increased thud of his heart; felt her own body's response.

While he kissed her she clung to him, returning each passionate embrace, jettisoning caution and self-preservation, feeding the desire that burned so hotly in him with her eager response to him.

As he kissed her he made a soft male sound of pleasure deep in his throat and then shifted the weight of his body from one foot to the other, pressing her intimately against him. Instead of re-coiling in rejection of his arousal, Miranda found that she was actually trying to move closer to him, arching her spine and moving her hips, but even her awareness of how dangerously she was behaving, even the knowledge that she had never behaved so wantonly, so foolishly in her whole life wasn't enough to stop her.

Ben's hands slid roughly down her body, shaping her hips then cupping her bottom, pulling her urgently into the heat and intimacy her senses so achingly sought.

It was an appeasement of the ache inside her of a kind, but it was not, she recognised tormentedly, enough. Not anywhere near enough.

While she was still trying to understand where it had come from, this need that burned so uncontrollably within her, Ben was kissing her throat, muttering words she could not distinguish into her skin, setting off small explosions of sharp pleasure where she felt the moist heat of his mouth on her flesh.

She was still clinging to him, but now, somehow or other, her hands were inside his jacket, pressed hard and flat against his shirt.

She heard Ben mutter something she couldn't comprehend, and then abruptly he was easing some space between them. While her deprived senses were still battling to accept the torment of losing her intimate physical contact with him, he was wrenching open the buttons on his shirt, seizing her hands, pushing them inside the unfastened garment and placing his own over them as he closed his eyes and shuddered visibly.

As he let go of her wrists and drew her back in his arms, he urged her, 'Touch me, Miranda. You can't know how much I want to feel your hands on my skin . . . your mouth . . .'

She shuddered herself, not sure if it was the heated erotic contact with his bare flesh that was responsible for own fierce upsurge in desire, or his husky passionate demands.

When he kissed her he groaned beneath his breath, his muscles straining against her, his skin so hot and damp where she touched him. She could feel the hardness of his nipples beneath her palm. When she moved her hand against him, he breathed in sharply, his breath rattling in his throat.

'Oh, God, Miranda.'

His hands were beneath her own top now, sliding round her ribcage, moulding the eager softness of her breasts, freeing them from the constriction of her bra.

She gasped out loud when he brushed her nipples with his fingers, helpless beneath the avalanche of need that rolled down over her.

She must have said something . . . asked something, but she had no idea what. All she heard was Ben's thick, fierce, 'Yes . . . Yes . . .' and then his mouth was on her breast, making her shudder with paroxysm after paroxysm of a pleasure so intense that she didn't think it was possible to survive it.

She heard herself call out his name, her voice raw and cracked. The answering pressure of his mouth against her breast made her shudder convulsively and swallow the sob of need that rose in her throat.

'Ben...Ben...' She couldn't stop herself any longer. She had to tell him how she felt about him...how much she loved him...wanted him.

Outside the kitchen window a small creature screamed, the sound of its death-cry cutting through their passion as sharply as a razor to a knot.

She felt Ben tense, and then slowly release her. As he stepped back from her, avoiding looking at her, she heard him apologising hoarsely, 'I'm sorry. That should never have happened. God, I thought I had more...more control.'

He sounded so conscience-stricken, so shocked, that Miranda winced, knowing that she had encouraged him, incited him...that the blame was not his alone, that she had shared his desire, even if he had not shared her love. *Her love*. She swallowed the sob that threatened to choke her, and said huskily, 'It wasn't your fault...I...'

'It should never have happened,' he repeated flatly. She realised as he turned towards her that he had fastened his shirt, but he had missed the top two buttons, and in the light she saw against his neck a scratch she was sure had not been there when he'd arrived.

Mortification and guilt turned her skin scarlet. She couldn't bear to look at him and had to turn her back to him.

'It shouldn't have happened,' he was repeating again. 'I should never have come here. God, Miranda, what can I say? I can only put it down to...to the emotional upset of the break-in.'

He had said nothing about her part in what had happened, and seemed determined to shoulder all the blame himself. Out of good manners, or because he had genuinely not realised? Not realised? How *could* he not have realised? she taunted herself. It was far more likely that he *had* realised and that by taking the blame he was trying subtly to warn her that what had happened should not have done so; that it had simply been a by-product of other emotions, and had no personal meaning for him. She had simply happened to be there. It had not been desire for *her* that had motivated him, simply a basic male need to find a means of releasing the tension and aggression of the evening.

'You don't need to say anything,' she told him shakily, still keeping her back to him. 'I think it's something we should both forget ever happened.'

He had gone very still, very tense almost. She could tell that without having to look round. Was this what love did to you—made you so achingly conscious of that beloved other that you could feel their changes of mood, almost as a physical reality?

Why was he so tense, though? This was what he wanted, wasn't it . . . to wipe out the events of the last hour as though they had never happened?

'I shouldn't have come here.' He seemed to be speaking more to himself than to her, and, in an effort to make things sound as normal as possible, Miranda said shakily, 'Well, at least no one's likely to have seen you, so it won't cause any more gossip.'

'So, you've heard the rumours as well, have you?'

She shrugged her shoulders.

'This is a small town. You're a newcomer, a single man. We were seen together at the golf club do, so people put two and two together and make twelve.'

She tried to sound casual and unconcerned. 'They'll soon find something else to talk about.'

'Yes,' Ben agreed flatly.

Miranda started to walk towards the door.

'I'm sorry Ralph is causing you so much trouble,' she told him as he followed her. 'He's a very dangerous man. He has a nasty temper.'

'He's also a coward,' Ben told her grimly. 'He sent others to do his dirty work for him.'

'Do you think he'll try again?' Miranda tried not to let her fear show in her voice.

'I don't think so,' Ben assured her. 'It would be too risky for him. He won't want to take the chance of people talking, pointing the finger in his direction. His sort never do.'

They had reached the front door, and as Miranda started to open it he touched her arm briefly and repeated, 'I'm sorry about...about tonight. I honestly had no intention when I came here——'

'No. I know,' Miranda interrupted him hastily, adding hesitantly, 'I think we're both mature enough to accept and understand that shock and trauma can cause all sorts of unlikely things to happen.'

She tensed as she realised that Ben was studying the book lying on the hall table. It was the book she had bought earlier in the day in Bath.

'You're interested in interpreting your dreams?' he asked her curiously.

Instantly she denied it, fibbing, 'It isn't mine. It belongs to a friend. She left it here.' She was starting to gabble, desperately trying to protect herself. And yet, why? If he hadn't realised from this evening just what kind of effect he had on her, he was scarcely likely to guess that she had bought the book in order to try to find some way of banishing her far too erotic dreams about him, was he?

After he had gone, Miranda went back to the kitchen and made herself a cup of coffee which she didn't drink. She then paced restlessly around the room, hugging her arms around her body as she tried to calm herself down. Tonight when she went to bed she was not going to dream about Ben. She was not going to dream about anyone or anything. She was going to sleep.

# CHAPTER SEVEN

'WELL, I must say that your father and Helen have been very lucky with the weather.'

'Very lucky,' Miranda responded stiltedly to Ben's comment. Ever since she had discovered that not only had Helen invited Ben to the wedding but that she had invited him to partner *her* as well, she had been so racked with discomfort that it had turned the day sour for her.

The sunshine which thrilled everyone else had given her a headache. The suit she had bought with so much pleasure had become something over-attention-seeking, a foolish bid to draw Ben's attention to her, and she felt uncomfortably self-conscious in it despite all the compliments she had received. If Helen hadn't asked Ben to partner her...

She gnawed miserably on her bottom lip. She had only found out about that this morning when Ben had telephoned her to ask her what time she wanted picking up. Until then she had had no idea that he was to be anything more than another wedding guest.

She had wanted to tell him that this pairing off of the two of them had nothing to do with her, but her pride wouldn't let her do so. He had already made it clear to her that he wasn't interested in her. If she had realised what Helen was doing...

The service was over, but there was still the reception to get through. It was being held at a country house hotel a few miles outside the town and Miranda, of course, without her own transport, would be obliged to travel there with Ben.

She had been all too conscious of the speculative attention they had been receiving, and now Ben, who had been talking to one of the other guests, turned back to her, and as though he had read her mind he murmured drily, 'I see a couple of your fellow committee members are watching us with avid interest. Are they going to be very disappointed, do you think, when they realise the truth?'

'Quite frankly I neither know nor care,' Miranda lied, flushing as she saw the way his eyebrows rose.

She was behaving like a spoiled, bad-tempered child, she knew, but instead of turning his back on her and ignoring her rudeness Ben frowned and asked with some concern, 'Are you all right? I noticed in the church that you looked pale.'

Yes, she had been pale. Pale with the strain of trying not to imagine that she and Ben were the ones exchanging their vows, here in the quiet coolness of this church where her own parents had married; where she herself had been christened. She was long past the stage of trying to deceive herself any longer about her feelings for him. She *couldn't* deny them and she certainly couldn't destroy them. She loved him.

'I...I have a bit of a headache,' she told him, avoiding looking at him. For some reason his concern made her want to cry. It would be so much easier to hold him at a distance if he were less warm-hearted, less concerned, less nice, she reflected miserably.

'Mm.' He was watching her closely. Too closely, she realised, as she looked up in an unguarded moment and met the warm concern of his eyes before her glance slid desperately away, afraid of what he might see in her eyes.

'You're not...? It isn't...?' He hesitated and then asked her quietly, 'You aren't upset about this marriage, are you?'

It took several seconds for his meaning to sink in, but once it had she responded immediately and vehemently.

'No...no, of course I'm not. I'm not a possessive child, Ben. I'm a woman.'

She knew as she'd said the word that it was a mistake, without quite knowing why. Ben was looking at her, watching her with an intensity that made her heart thud heavily.

'A woman. Yes, you certainly are that,' he agreed slowly.

For some reason his words made her flush and rush into nervous speech. 'I'm *glad* they're getting married. I'm very happy for them, for *both* of them.'

'So, if it wasn't your father's marriage that was making you look so...so unhappy during the service, what was it?'

She caught her breath. She had never dreamed that Ben might have been watching her, might have been aware... She hunted wildly for something to say, but before she could speak an old acquaintance of her father's came up to her and took hold of her hand, patting it.

'This is a very happy day for your father,' he told her, 'and yet I couldn't help thinking when we were in church about your mother...'

As he left them, Ben said quickly, 'I'm sorry; I should have realised. Of course, you would have been thinking about your mother.'

'Yes, a little,' Miranda agreed, trying not to feel uncomfortable. It was true she had thought of her mother, but only with the knowledge of how pleased she would have been to know that they were happy; but if she told Ben the truth he might keep on pressing her, wanting to know why she had been upset, and she could hardly tell him the real reason, could she? She could hardly blurt out that her misery had been caused by the admission of her love for him and its hopelessness.

The ceremony, the wedding breakfast, the speeches—all of them had gone off very well, everyone agreed as they gathered together outside the hotel to wave the bridal couple off. Miranda's head was still aching, but for Helen and her father's sake she tried not to let it show.

As she went forward to kiss her new stepmother and hug her father, Jeffrey Shepherd said quickly, 'Good heavens, I nearly forgot! Ben was asking me if I could find out anything about a house he's seen and fancied. It's empty at the moment—owner died a while back. I've managed to track down the solicitors dealing with it, the estate wants to sell, and a covering letter plus the keys will be coming through the post in a few days' time, once they've got everything sorted out. Be a good girl, will you, Miranda, and make sure Ben gets the keys as soon as they arrive? He's pretty anxious to have a look at this place.'

Before he could say any more they were being overwhelmed by well-wishers and hurried into the waiting car, while Miranda controlled her exasperation and her curiosity.

Once the bridal couple had gone, everyone else started to leave. Miranda—who had promised Helen she would collect her bouquet and take it home with her, along with the suitcases containing their wedding finery—suggested to Ben that he might prefer her to get a taxi back rather than keep him waiting.

'Not at all,' he told her promptly. 'I'm not doing anything else this evening. In fact——'

He broke off as the vicar's wife came up to them and started chatting to him. Leaving him to it, Miranda hurried back into the hotel to collect everything. As she crossed the lobby and headed for the stairs, she saw Ralph Charlesworth coming down them towards her. It was too late for her to take evasive action and so she stayed where she was.

Ralph was swaying slightly as he walked, and as he drew level with her Miranda could smell the spirit on his breath.

'Looking for me, darling?' he leered, making a grab for her but luckily missing.

'No, I'm not,' Miranda told him shortly.

'No, you wouldn't be, would you?' he agreed sourly. 'Got other fish to fry now, haven't you?

Well, if you think I'm still going to want you once he's kicked you out of his bed——'

'Everything all right, darling?'

Miranda froze as she heard Ben's voice. As she turned her head, he came up behind her, resting his arm protectively against her back as he confronted Ralph.

To Miranda's relief, Ralph said nothing, but as he walked past them, either by accident or deliberately he pushed into Ben, virtually trying to elbow him out of the way.

'Appalling manners that man has,' another guest commented disapprovingly as Ralph walked away.

'He's obviously had far too much to drink,' his female companion added.

'You OK?' Ben asked her quietly.

She nodded her head. 'Fine. I'll just go upstairs and check that the cases are ready to come down and then we can go.'

'Want me to come with you?'

His thoughtfulness made her throat ache. She had never known before that a man could be both so strong and so tender.

'No. I'll be all right.'

Half an hour later when they were eventually ready to leave, Miranda frowned as she saw Ralph's new Jaguar careering far too fast down the hotel drive.

'Ralph isn't *driving* is he?' she commented to Ben.

'I'm afraid so. When I went to get the car, he and his wife were in the car park having a row about it. The man's a fool. If he gets stopped by the police... not to mention the danger he is to other road-users. Perhaps I should have intervened, but somehow I didn't think any comment from me would be well received.'

'If I were Susan, I'd have refused to go with him,' Miranda said roundly.

As Ben set his own car in motion, she smothered a yawn, her lack of sleep caused either by the hours she spent lying awake thinking about Ben, and worrying about what she suspected was fast becoming a helpless addiction to him, or by the powerfully erotic dreams she had when she did sleep.

He was a good driver, making it easy for her to relax in the car. A tape played soothingly as she eased herself back in her seat, closing her eyes. She wasn't going to sleep, of course. Just resting her eyes for a few minutes...

'Miranda.'

The warm male voice whispering her name penetrated her sleep. She had heard it whisper her name so often before in her dreams that her response to it was immediate and effortless.

As she started to wake up, she turned towards it, her mouth curving into a soft smile, her body stretching voluptuously.

'Ben.'

She said his name softly, with the drowsy certainty of the pleasure it gave her to say it, in the same way she had already tasted his skin. Her eyes opened and focused languorously on his face. He was too far away from her. They should have been lying so closely together that when he breathed she could feel the movement of his chest, the exhalation of his breath. She started to frown, ready to chide him for being so distant, and then abruptly her brain realised the truth.

*This* was no dream: this was reality. Another second and she would have betrayed herself completely, reaching for Ben, telling him ... begging him ...

She shuddered involuntarily.

They were, she realised now, parked outside her house. She had obviously drifted off to sleep and slept for longer and far more deeply than she had realised, hence that disturbing confusion when she had woken up between what was real, and what was merely a product of her over-active dreaming subconscious.

'I'm sorry if I startled you,' she heard Ben saying.

'*I'm* sorry I fell asleep,' she countered.

'I had intended to suggest that perhaps we might have dinner together, but in the circumstances...'

Dinner with Ben? Would her self-control hold up under a strain of that magnitude?

She gave another tiny shiver.

'You're cold. I'd better get these cases inside for you and leave you in peace.'

In peace? Miranda doubted that she would ever know that state of mind again.

'If you give me your keys, I'll go and unlock the door first.'

She wanted to protest that there was no need, that she was not some fragile feminine Victorian maiden in need of cherishing and protecting; but instead she found she was reaching automatically for her handbag and removing the keys.

As she handed them to him, he bent towards her, his fingers brushing hers.

She went completely still, her mouth dry, her heart beating frantically and shallowly.

If just such a brief non-sexual touch could affect her so intensely, what would it be like if...?

Betrayingly her glance focused on his mouth, and even more betrayingly stayed there, her own lips parting.

Now he too had gone very still.

'Miranda.'

Something in his voice compelled her to shift her concentration from his mouth to his eyes. They had gone very dark, very intense. The way he was looking at her made her catch her breath and openly give way to the tiny shiver of sensation that gripped her body. There was nothing remotely non-sexual about the way he was looking at her now. In fact...

His fingers tightened over hers, hot colour suddenly washing over her skin.

He bent his head towards her. She couldn't drag her glance away from his, from the openly sexual message she could read in it.

Her heart started to race, adrenalin flooding her nervous system as her senses responded to the silent messages of his.

When his hand slid into her hair and cupped the back of her head, angling it so that he could kiss her, she didn't try to resist.

When his lips touched hers, she trembled, only just suppressing the desire to curl her fingers into his jacket and hold on to him.

He kissed her gently, as though savouring the texture of her lips, their softness, their warmth; their responsiveness to him.

It was a slow, unhurried exploration, and yet for all that she felt an almost violent urge to press herself close against him, to open her mouth beneath his and invite the deep penetrating invasion of his tongue, to wind her arms around him and . . .

A frantic sob of terror built up inside her chest as she realised what was happening to her. She drew back from him as though his touch were corrosive, causing the tenderness in his eyes to give way to cool withdrawal.

'I'm sorry,' he apologised. 'I thought——'

'It was my fault,' Miranda interrupted him, her face flaming. She could well imagine *what* he had thought. After all, hadn't she by her own action virtually invited . . . incited . . . encouraged him to respond to her own desire for him? 'I must go in. I've delayed you long enough.' She was starting to gabble frantically, guilt and embarrassment sharpened by the pangs of longing and love tearing her apart inside.

She didn't look at him as he carried the cases inside for her, nor did she suggest that he might like to stay for a cup of coffee.

When he had finally driven off, she told herself that she was glad he hadn't repeated his invitation to have dinner with him, but long after he had gone, when she really ought to have been doing half a dozen far more practical and essential things, she found that she was standing motionless in her kitchen, remembering how it had felt to have his mouth tenderly caressing her own, and how the sensation that that gentle touch had evoked had made her quiver inside with longing and need. She was even doing it now, the ache in her body intensifying and spreading to such an extent that she almost groaned out aloud. Her fingers touched her mouth and she closed her eyes, torn between helpless despair and frustrated self-anger.

What was she doing to herself, torturing herself like this?

The fact that her father was away and that in his absence she was so very busy should have made it not just easy, but also very necessary for Miranda to shut Ben and her love for him out of her mind completely, but unfortunately this did not prove to be the case.

Three days after the wedding, exhausted by repeated dreams about him—in which her treacherous imagination allowed him access to the kind of intimate fantasies which were doing absolutely nothing to reinforce her need to face reality and to accept that, while just like any other man, though he might respond sexually to the wanton provocation of her own desire, he did not and never would share the love she had for him—she finally gave in. After returning from the office, instead of concentrating on the work she had brought home for herself, she picked up the book she had bought on the interpretation of dreams, and started to study it.

What she read in its pages didn't tell her anything she had not already known, although it did have some helpful tips on how to redirect the course of nightmares or unpleasant dreams so that they became non-threatening. Maybe that would work for her: if she mentally tried to substitute another man for Ben, or found some way to redirect their dream encounters so that they became harmless and non-sexual.

It was worth a try at least. She certainly could not go on like this, afraid to go to sleep in case she dreamed about him, growing more and more tired, and with less and less resistance to her dreams when she could no longer force herself to stay awake.

She hadn't seen or heard anything of Ben, and she told herself that she was glad, and yet, when she arrived at work four days after the wedding to discover that the keys had arrived for the property Ben wanted to view, her immediate feeling was one of joy that she now had a legitimate reason to get in touch with him.

However, when several telephone calls and a hesitant lunchtime visit to the house on the High Street had not brought her in contact with him, she confided to Liz that she suspected he must be in London.

As she nibbled tentatively on her bottom lip, she told her, 'The problem is that Dad was most insistent that Ben—Mr Frobisher wanted the keys as soon as they arrived.'

'Well, you could always drive over there and post them through his letter-box if he isn't in,' Liz commented reasonably.

'Mm.' That solution had occurred to Miranda as well, and yet, for all her yearning need to see him, perhaps in fact *because* of it, she was reluctant to do so. In case he wasn't there, or in case he was?

She was becoming tired of her own irrational behaviour, she acknowledged later that day, when she had stayed at her desk until gone seven to catch up on the backlog of paperwork her father's absence had inevitably caused.

She looked at the phone and then picked up the receiver, but when she dialled Ben's number, once again there was no response.

Closing her eyes, she asked herself what she would have done if he had simply been another client and not one—she swallowed painfully, forcing herself to frame the words that felt as though they were written in fire inside her—not one with whom she was quite desperately in love.

She already knew the answer, of course. She would have driven over to the client's house and dropped the keys along with an explanatory note through his or her letter-box.

Make sure Ben gets the keys as soon as they arrive, her father had said.

Sighing faintly to herself, she scribbled a hasty covering letter and sealed it, together with the keys, in an envelope, and then, having collected her jacket, she picked up her bag, locked up the office and headed for her car.

All the way over to the cottage Ben was renting, she told herself that he wasn't going to be there; that there was no reason for her heartbeat to pick up, nor her pulse to race so frantically; that there was no reason for her to feel this sick coiling excitement tightening her stomach; this guilt, this anger against herself for her own weakness.

When she reached the cottage, she stopped her car, and before getting out forced herself to take several deep, supposedly calming breaths, but all they did was make her in danger of hyper-ventilating, increasing the flutter of nerves gripping her stomach and making her shake with tension when she finally managed to get out of the car and walk towards the door.

She knocked on it hesitantly, and then, when there was no answer, a little more forcefully.

She was just about to open the letter-box and push the envelope into it when she heard Ben call out from behind the closed door, 'Hang on. I shan't be a sec.'

And then there was the sound of a bolt being drawn back, and a lock being unfastened, and Ben was opening the door.

When she saw him standing there in the hallway, for a moment she was too overwrought to even speak. He was wearing a bathrobe, and his hair was damp—his body too, she realised as her glance slid helplessly down over his robe-clad body and focused on the beads of water tangling damply in the dark hair that furred his legs.

Her own legs had abruptly and disconcertingly turned to jelly, so that she was helpless to do anything other than stand there trembling as he came towards her, practically thrusting the small package containing her note and the keys at him just as soon as he came within reach of her.

'I've brought you the keys for the property you wanted to see,' she told him quickly, so unnerved by the sight of him, by the realisation that he was probably completely naked beneath his robe and that she must have disturbed him while he was having his shower, that her voice became high and strained, her words falling over one another in her haste to have them said and be free to take her leave of him. 'Dad said to get them to you as soon as they arrived. I did try to telephone...'

'I've been in London today,' he told her calmly. 'Thanks for going to so much trouble.'

As he took the packet from her, for some reason he caught hold of her wrist as well, circling it with fingers that were damp and cool. She could feel her pulse accelerate into frantic betrayal as she tensed herself against her awareness of him. His thumb was pressed against her pulse. She knew he must be able to measure its desperate race. Unwittingly she made a small choking sound of distress in her throat as his thumb rubbed contemplatively against her pulse in an action which she had no doubt was meant to be soothing, but which in reality...

She tried to take a deep, relaxing breath and found that she couldn't because her muscles were clenched so tight, and while she fought for breath and composure he tugged firmly on her wrist, saying easily, 'Come inside. I was just going to make myself a cup of coffee. If you've got time to have one with me, you could help me unravel this untranslateable estate agent's jargon.'

Several different emotions clamoured for supremacy inside her, all of them so powerful and so distracting that he had practically dragged her into the hall and closed the door behind her before she knew what was happening.

She opened her mouth to tell him firmly and professionally that she was quite sure a man of his intelligence was capable of interpreting an estate agent's brochure without her assistance, but at that moment he chose to turn towards her, standing so close to her that she inadvertently breathed in the clean soapy smell of his skin. Her heart felt as though it was literally bouncing around inside her ribcage, even though she knew such an occurrence was physically impossible, and, instead of speaking to him as she had intended, she found that she was rimming the dry outline of her parted lips with betraying nervous darts of her tongue-tip.

'Mm. You smell good.'

The intimate compliment, so unexpected, so closely mirrored her own shocked, private awareness of how much the clean damp scent of his skin made her want to reach out and touch him, to run her fingertips along the edges and open lapels of his robe, to slide her hands inside it and to press her palms flat against his chest, to touch her mouth to the strong column of his throat and let her tongue lap delicately at the tiny beads of moisture clinging there.

This was madness...complete insanity. She took a deep, shuddering breath and then another, ignoring his compliment, wondering a little bitterly if he had any idea at all of what he was doing to her, or the havoc he was wreaking on her emotions, her desires... her whole life.

It was abnormal... immoral... obscene almost, surely, for a woman to have such erotic and intimate thoughts about a man who was little more than an acquaintance... a man, moreover, who had done nothing at all to encourage or give rise to such thoughts. Well, very little, she amended, trying not to think about how he had kissed her.

'I... I don't really want any coffee,' she started to tell him, making a desperate bid to assert herself and banish the wildness of her private thoughts.

'No,' he agreed thoughtfully, his thumb resting deliberately against her frantic pulse. 'Perhaps you have already received more than enough stimulation for one day.'

For a moment she thought he had actually guessed what was happening to her; had even perhaps looked into her mind and seen the desires... the need... the love she was trying so desperately to control.

The horror of it held her motionless and silent.

'Not had another run-in with Charlesworth, have you?'

She almost shook with relief, and told him huskily, 'No... nothing like that... I suppose it's just the strain of Dad being away.'

She blinked suddenly as Ben pushed open the kitchen door. She hadn't realised they had moved, but they must have done, and now, as he ushered her inside, he released her wrist.

'I'm sure you don't really need my help——' she began, but Ben interrupted her, telling her softly, 'I wanted to show you the details, talk over with you some of my plans for the house if I manage to get it. It's very old, Tudor, with a later Queen Anne façade and frontage. I found it quite by chance and fell in love with it.'

Miranda had in fact already seen the details, unable to resist taking a peek at them, and the potential of the house had made her envy his ability to buy it.

'It . . . it sounds lovely,' she told him, her voice even more husky than his. 'But I shouldn't really stay.'

He had had his back to her, but now he turned round and saw the way her colour rose and fell as she gestured helplessly towards him.

'I obviously interrupted you.'

'I was having a shower, that's all.' He was watching her closely, too closely, she recognised nervously. 'I'll put the kettle on. We'll have tea instead of coffee. Better for us both.'

As he walked away from her, her glance followed him, hungrily, hopelessly. She could feel her eyes stinging with the intensity of her emotional pain as she was torn between her love for him, and the anger and self-contempt that the vulnerability within her always evoked. She felt so helpless, so weak . . . so out of control.

She watched as he filled the kettle, almost shaking with the tension of trying to deny what she was feeling.

If he were to turn to her now, to take her in his arms, to kiss her...to touch her as he had done last night in her dream, sliding the clothes from her body, praising the feminine responsiveness of it as he stroked and kissed her skin, his mouth lingering achingly on the soft curves of her breasts, on the trembling tautness of her belly, on her thighs, while her hands—— She couldn't suppress the anguished moan that tore at her throat.

Ben heard it and turned round immediately, concern furrowing his forehead.

'What is it? What's wrong?' he asked her, coming over to her. She had to sit down. She couldn't stand up a second longer, she felt so weak, so terrified of what was happening to her.

She dropped down into a chair, shivering from head to foot, feeling her skin overheat and then chill in reaction to her desire for him.

Ben dropped on his knees beside her, so close to her that his robe gaped slightly as he moved.

'What is it? What's wrong?' he demanded again.

She couldn't stand it a moment longer. Everything that she was suffering welled up inside her, and before she could stop herself she burst out frantically, 'It's you. It's... Oh, for heaven's sake, can't you put some clothes on...?'

## CHAPTER EIGHT

THE silence stretching between them crackled with electricity, with tension, with pain almost.

'Put some clothes on?' Ben repeated slowly.

He withdrew from her, standing up, watching her. She knew he was watching her, but she couldn't bring herself to look back at him.

What on earth had she done? Why on earth had she said it?

'Is *that* what's wrong? Am *I* the one causing all this?' he demanded grimly, reaching for her wrist, and trapping it before she could move, his thumb pressing down deliberately hard on the fast race of her pulse. 'Is *that* the reason you tense up every time I come within a yard of you...because you find me so——'

'Irresistible.' The high hard-sounding word hurt her throat and twisted her mouth, but she had to say it herself before he threw it at her. She had never felt more humiliated...more vulnerable in all her life, and yet at the same time there was a curious sense of light-headedness, relief almost, in finally admitting to him just what she was going through. She felt like someone who had carefully avoided danger all their lives and yet now, confronted with it, was deliberately abandoning themselves to it.

'Irresistible?' There was an odd note in his voice. '*I* was going to say just the opposite.'

She flinched visibly, her shock showing clearly in the defensive movement of her body. Had he really thought that...that she found him physically repugnant...that she...?

'Irresistible...' He said the word softly, marvellingly almost, and yet, for all the softness of his voice, it still jarred unbearably on her too-sensitive nerves.

'Please.' She tried to stand up and then realised that if she did she would be standing right next to him, so she subsided back into her chair, turning her face away from him as she pleaded huskily, 'I don't want to talk about it. I...'

'Oh, but I do.' She gave him one frantic, panicky glance but he ignored it, repeating again, 'Irresistible.'

This time it seemed as though he was savouring the word, enjoying it, drawing it out and with it her agony.

'*How* irresistible?' he questioned her, bending towards her.

If he touched her now she would disintegrate completely, she knew it, and yet she wasn't going to get out of here until she had answered his question—she knew that as well—and it was far, far more than she could cope with.

Hating herself for her weakness and him for his strength, she buried her face in her hands and told him in a tormented whisper, 'How am I supposed to define that? By degrees? A little bit irresistible . . . sort of irresistible? Well, if you want the truth . . .' She took a deep, shuddering breath and found it was of no use: nothing was going to stop the avalanche of emotion building up inside it; it was going to roll down over her and destroy her no matter what she tried to do to avoid it. She could either try and outrun it or stay and face it, confront it . . . accept it . . . admit it.

With her face still buried in her hands, she began rawly, 'Well, if I told you that virtually ever since we met I've been——' She stopped and swallowed. She *couldn't* do this . . . couldn't strip her soul and her heart bare for him like this . . . reveal her innermost and deeply private emotions and needs to him like this, and yet if she didn't he would question and probe until he had dragged every last nugget of information from her.

'You've been what?' Ben pressed, confirming her panicky thoughts.

In a voice thick with self-loathing, she told him sickly, 'I've been having these . . . these dreams . . . about . . . about you. About . . .' She shuddered helplessly, unable to go on, unable to admit to him the full enormity of what had been happening to her.

She felt his hand touch her shoulder, his breath warm her ear. 'Look at me, Miranda,' he urged her, but she couldn't . . . couldn't bear to confront the pity and revulsion she knew must be in his eyes.

And yet, when he said huskily, 'You aren't alone, you know,' she immediately did just what she had been determined not to do, and dropped her hands from her face, lifting it so that she could look at him.

If it was the hesitant, almost tortured sound of his voice that compelled her to look at him, then it was the expression of wry self-mockery in his eyes that kept her attention on him.

'You aren't alone, you know,' he repeated softly. 'I have dreams too.'

'I don't believe you,' she denied shakily.

His mouth compressed.

'No?' he countered tautly. 'Well, how about this, then? Last night, for instance, I dreamed that instead of leaving me after the wedding you came back here with me, and that when I kissed you the way I'd been aching to kiss you all day, with your mouth soft and open beneath mine, with your body warm and eager in my arms, that when I kissed you, you whispered to me that you needed and wanted me, and I picked you up and carried you upstairs to my bed, where I undressed you and touched and kissed every exquisite inch of your skin. I can still remember just how you looked and felt. It's been tormenting me all day, driving me out of my mind, making me ache in a way I haven't done since I was sixteen,' he told her fiercely, ignoring her frantic husky denial of what he was telling her, pressing on inexorably.

'Shall I tell you how soft your skin was, how warm, how wonderfully feminine, or shall I tell you about the way you cried out my name when I gave in to my need to be a little rough . . . a little violent, when it wasn't enough just to touch and kiss the soft scented mystery of your body, when I had to suck and bite, and you, instead of reproaching me for my urgency, made soft delirious sounds of pleasure in your throat and clung to me, wanting me, driving me wild with the sweet passionate sound of your love cries and the way you clung to me, your hands...?

'Shall I tell you what you did with your hands, Miranda? Shall I tell you how you touched me, stroked me, aroused me, until I was mad with the need to have you, to penetrate the sweet sanctuary of your body, to feel it welcome and envelop me, drawing me so deeply within it that I knew when the final moment of release came that I had touched the innermost core of you?

'Have you *any* idea what it feels like for a man, knowing that ... knowing that a woman wants and needs him so much that she allows him that degree of intimacy?'

They were both trembling, Miranda realised as she felt the deep vibration that ran from her own body to his. She could still scarcely comprehend what he was telling her, scarcely believe what she was hearing, even though her body had already responded shockingly to it, so that a slow sweet ache was spilling relentlessly through her, carrying its drugging intoxication to every part of her.

'And then, later,' Ben told her hoarsely, 'later when I had held you and told you how awed you'd made me feel, how very much a man...' He paused, his mouth twisting with self-mockery. 'Do you realise that before this I'd always thought myself too intelligent, too cerebral to concern myself with such outdated, almost macho feelings, but perhaps our dreams reveal far more of ourselves than our conscious minds will ever allow, and I certainly can't deny that in *my* dreams the feeling of being super-human almost, even, dare I say it, super-male...a feeling fuelled by your responsiveness to me...your complete and total acceptance of me, was so strong, so unforgettable, that it lingered even longer than my awareness that the degree of pleasure I'd shared with you was something I've never experienced in real life. Just as the fact that having made love with you so intensely and intimately once did not prevent me from repeating the experience, not once but twice in that same dream sequence, is also something I've never managed and, if I'm honest, never desired to do in real life, but in my dream, the moment your hands touched my skin, the moment you started kissing my throat, stroking my body...' He paused, and Miranda saw that there were small tiny beads of sweat clinging to his forehead, and for some odd reason that, more than anything else he had said to her, finally convinced her that he was speaking the truth; that he was not simply tormenting her out of some crazy desire to amuse himself at her expense.

'When...when I kissed you...what?'

Her voice sounded strained and husky. It wobbled slightly as well, but at least she had managed to speak, even if Ben was shaking his head and telling her roughly, 'What did you do next? That's something I can't bring myself to tell you...'

His mouth twisted again as he looked at her and told her bluntly, 'And not just because it would shock the life out of you. It damn near shocked the life out of me.'

'What did?' Miranda demanded almost aggressively. 'That a woman like me with almost no experience...a woman who doesn't date...who doesn't... That a woman like me should actually *want* to show a man how much she...likes him...how much she desires him...how much she wants to give him the same pleasure he's been giving her, no matter how shockingly intimate that pleasure might be? Is that what you think about my sex, that there's a certain kind of woman who's *allowed* to express her sexuality, her desire, and then another kind like me who isn't——' She broke off abruptly. What was happening to her...what was she saying...thinking? Ben had been talking about a dream...not reality.

'Would you want to...to share that kind of intimacy with a man, Miranda? To feel his hands and his mouth caressing you so intimately? Would *you* want to caress him as intimately, to let him feel the silken softness of your lips against his flesh, soothing its heat and ardour at the same time as they incited it?'

The kitchen suddenly seemed to have become far too hot, Miranda discovered, and the top button of her shirt too tight, constricting her breath.

She was aware that the spreading ache inside her body had become an almost frighteningly urgent pulse.

She licked her too-dry lips and said huskily, 'I...I...don't want to talk about it any more. I...'

'You what?' Ben demanded rawly. 'You want to run away and hide yourself from the truth?'

Her eyelids flickered, her face going pale. What did he mean by the truth? Had he *guessed* that she loved him? Had he...?

'Do you think it's just possible that our mutual subconsciouses are waging a war against us, Miranda, and trying to tell our conscious minds something they seem to want to ignore?'

Her heart was thudding so heavily it was practically a physical pain. She focused numbly on him, her eyes huge and haunted. He looked tired, drawn, as though what he had said to her had drained him emotionally and physically; it could not have been easy for him, she recognised. No man liked admitting he was vulnerable, especially not to a woman, especially not to the woman who was the cause of that vulnerability.

She wetted her dry lips again, heat burning her skin as she caught the way he was watching her; felt the smouldering burn of his concentration on her face...on her mouth. Without being able to do a thing about it, she felt her lips soften and swell slightly. She tried to compress them together, horrifiedly realising that they were almost forming a pout, almost willing him to respond to their provocation by...

She tried frantically to redirect her thoughts but found them sliding helplessly into even more dangerous channels...her hands against his skin, her lips. She closed her eyes and realised at once that it was a mistake. In the darkness behind her shuttered lids, she was far too vulnerable to the erotic images of her rebellious thoughts.

'What is it, Miranda?'

Ben's breath against her ear was pure torment, as dangerous to her self-control as though he had taken her in his arms and destroyed it with the fierce stamp of his kiss. 'Does the intimacy of your dreams disturb you as much as mine do me? Does it haunt and beguile your waking hours? Do you find yourself caught between your logical waking need to suppress such thoughts, such needs, such dreams, and your sleeping desire to allow yourself the freedom you could never permit your waking self?

'You speak of there being two kinds of women, but those are *your* thoughts, not mine. Perhaps *you* are the one who believes that for some reason you cannot allow yourself——'

'No. No, that's not true. *You're* the one who said you couldn't.'

'Not because I categorise you into a certain pre-set mould, but because I felt you had every right to be both offended and angry that in my dreams I had virtually compelled you into an act of intimacy which should only be shared, given and taken with mutual wanting and respect.'

Respect. Miranda savoured the word shakily. It seemed an odd choice for him to have made, especially when the intimacy they were discussing...

She felt her skin burn, not just her whole face, but her body as well, and heard Ben saying curtly, 'You see? Even talking about it embarrasses you, so how the hell do you think I feel? And not just because of the way my dream self made love to you...not just because of the intimacies we shared. How the hell do you think it's been for me? Looking at you, and remembering; looking at your mouth and thinking...aching...helpless to do a damned thing about it, even while I'm cursing myself for my lack of self-control?'

'It's been the same for me.'

She had blurted out the admission before she could stop herself, torn between shame and relief; shame at what she was admitting and relief that she was not alone; that there was after all someone who shared and understood the appalling nature of this self-inflicted torture.

'You know why all this is happening, don't you?' Ben demanded grimly.

She held her breath, her body tensing. Was he going to say that it was her fault...that it was somehow caused by the fact that she had fallen so deeply in love with him, that she was in some in-direct and unfathomable way giving his body some kind of message which translated into the dreams they were both suffering?

Without waiting for her to reply, he continued angrily, 'I know you won't like hearing this and I'm damned sure you're not going to admit it, but I submit that the reason we're both suffering these dreams is because, despite all the evidence to the contrary, physically at least we're very much attracted to one another.'

Miranda's brain flinched from what he was saying; from the fact that, while he spoke of need and desire, he made no mention of love, and yet at the same time she was relieved: relieved that he hadn't after all guessed her secret. Attracted to one another, he had said...physically, at least.

'Nothing to say?' His voice jarred, hurting something soft and vulnerable inside her.

'What am I supposed to say?' she asked him tightly. 'Yes, you're right, let's jump into bed and have sex with one another? Who knows, perhaps the reality will be so very different from our dreams, so disappointing that it will cure us of them for good?'

There was a long pause. Miranda looked doggedly into space, angry with both him and with herself. She was over-reacting, behaving like a child, but she couldn't help it, she was afraid—afraid of the helpless longing beating inside her, a longing which told her that once he touched her, held her, loved her, even if that loving was only physical, only sex, she would never ever be able to return to the person she had been before; that a part of her would be destroyed, held in bondage forever; that she would never again be completely whole...completely her own person. She was afraid of the intimacy of loving him, of the awesome power of it, of the commitment she knew she would be helpless to stop herself from giving him, and yet hadn't she already made a far deeper, and far more dangerous commitment in allowing herself to fall in love with him in the first place? *Allowing* herself... She bit down hard on her bottom lip.

'Is *that* what you think—that the reality is bound to be disappointing... to fall so far short of our dreams that it will make us both wish we had left things as they were?

'Is *that* your previous experience of loving someone intimately, Miranda?'

There was such a quiet sadness in his voice that it made her eyes sting with painful tears.

'My previous experience of sex,' she told him fiercely, stressing the word 'sex', refusing the anodyne of his soft-voiced 'loving someone intimately', 'is restricted to the extremely humiliating and rather less than pleasant half-hour I spent with the boy to whom I lost my virginity. I was twenty. He was twenty-three. We met on holiday. I'd grown tired of wondering what it was all about, of wanting to know and knowing that there was no way I could find out, not living here... not with anyone I knew... not unless I was prepared to take the same route my girlfriends were taking—going steady, getting engaged, married... having children. I *didn't* want that... and, as I quickly and probably very well deservedly, rather painfully found out, I didn't want the kind of cheap encounter I'd invited by encouraging Ricky.'

'Did you love him?'

The harsh question almost seemed accusatory. She flinched from it but shook her head, glaring at him as she demanded, 'Did you love the first girl you had sex with? Can you even remember her?'

'I was seventeen. She was twenty. I found out later she had seduced me for a bet,' he told her drily. 'Does that answer your question? After that I was extremely selective about allowing myself to get involved in any intimate relationships. If I can't honestly say that, yes, I loved the few women I've been intimate with, then at least I *can* say that at the outset, when the relationship was new, I believed I *could* love them and that that love could be returned. I suspect I was rather too intense for them. It took me a long time to realise that modern women relished their independence and did not, as my mother had done, believe that true fulfillment came from falling in love with a man and having his babies. As I said, I was rather too intense and certainly very immature. I know better now, and fully appreciate that a woman needs her independence, her career...that she has a right to direct her own life, and that it *is* possible to combine marriage, a career and motherhood, provided both partners are willing to share the responsibilities and burdens that go with that kind of commitment.'

'You consider children to be a burden?' Miranda challenged.

He looked at her for a long time and then said steadily, 'No, I don't. Just as I would never carelessly or without thought cause a woman to conceive my child. Unless...' He stopped, looking at her with such an unfathomable expression, with such heat...with such intensity that she had to clench her body against the reaction to it, biting instinctively and deeply into her bottom lip. 'For God's sake, don't do that.'

The harsh command confused her. She looked at him uncertainly.

'Don't you *know* what it makes a man want to do when he sees a woman he already desires...aches for, doing that? Don't you *know* how it makes him want to soothe the soft swelling caused by that small sharp pressure with his tongue, with his mouth, that need driving him to such a pitch that *he* becomes the one savaging that softness, using its sensitivity to make her cry out with passion and need of her own, and invite him to penetrate the sweet depths of her mouth, to hold her body against his, to let *her* feel all that she's making *him* feel...how she's making him ache? Just the way *you're* making me ache right now, Miranda.'

'No.' Her own senses recognised that it was more a moan of acquiescence than a denial, but it stopped him. Momentarily at least, long enough for her to get stumblingly to her feet, and to attempt to step past him. This had gone on long enough. She had to leave, now, while she still had the will-power to do so, but, as she made to move past him, her feet became unusually clumsy. She hesitated, stumbled, and fell awkwardly against him, clutching instinctively at the open lapels of his robe, while he moved forward just as instinctively to catch her, both of them unaware that her instinctive grab for his robe had caused the slack knot in its belt to unravel, leaving only the thinness of her own clothes as a barrier between them as he caught her up against him, not out of desire or lust, but simply out of an automatic and wholly male chivalric response to her plight, her weakness, she recognised as she clung dizzily to his robe and allowed herself to savour her intimacy with him. Just for a second...a minute. It could, after all, do no harm. She would soon be gone, and never again...

As though in defiance of what she was thinking, her body willfully pressed closer and then trembled at its own audacity.

In her ear, Ben muttered sharply, warningly, 'Miranda, don't.'

She turned her head to retaliate untruthfully that she had done nothing, at the same moment that he turned his. Her eyes were almost level with his mouth. She watched it helplessly, seeing it frame something she could no longer hear, no longer wanted to hear.

When she touched it with her fingertips he trembled, and so did she. She could have withdrawn from him then, should have done so, but she didn't. She told herself later that the reason she had pressed her fingertips so briefly to his mouth had been because she wanted to stop them from trembling and not because—as he seemed to believe—she had wanted him to open his mouth and to slowly and shockingly draw her fingers inside it, sucking on them, licking them so slowly and lingeringly that, long before he had gripped her wrist and removed her damp fingers from his mouth so that his lips could caress her palm and then her wrist, she had forgotten why she had got to her feet in the first place…that she had ever intended to leave, that she had ever intended to do anything other than stand here with her body pressed against him, trembling and shaking as though she had a fever, small mewing sounds clogging her throat as he showed her just how pale and shadowed were her dreams when compared with reality.

# CHAPTER NINE

WHEN he kissed her, her response to him turned the caressive pressure of his mouth into a fierce driving heat that made her feel as though her bones had melted, as though her body had become soft and pliant like ivy, clinging and twining with its more solidly muscled host until the two of them grew as one.

Ben's hands were in her hair, holding her a willing captive beneath his mouth as he opened hers, incited to do so by the hungry impatient passion of her small teeth biting at his bottom lip.

As his tongue stroked into her mouth his hands spread across her scalp, his fingers flexing in the same deeply rhythmical motion as his tongue, his whole body, she recognised as she instinctively matched the fierce rotation of his hips, pressing herself closer to him, offering him the subtly complementary rhythm of her own desire, hot darts of sensation thrilling through her body when it welcomed his arousal, his need, his passion.

'If this doesn't stop right now, it won't stop until I've taken you to bed, and spent all night making love to you.'

The husky words were whispered against her ear, as Ben dragged his mouth from hers. She could feel the hard rapid thud of his heart as though it were trying to break out of his body and invade her own. She could see the slickness of sweat dampening his skin, feel the fine tremble that shook his straining muscles.

She shivered wildly, her body aching in response to the images conjured up by her mind, images of the two of them together, in the warm darkness of his bed, of their bodies joyously entwined. She could even hear the harsh labour of their breathing, knew how his flesh would taste; how his body would feel beneath her hands, within her own.

His mouth caressed the soft arch of her throat. If she didn't want this to continue, now was the time to tell him so... now was the time to let sanity take hold and direct her.

She could feel the control he was striving to exercise, sense the withdrawal he was about to make. She pressed closer to him, sliding her hands inside his robe and over his shoulders, her nails digging into his flesh as she begged, 'No... don't stop. Not now.'

She could feel his tension. He raised his head and looked at her, and when she would have avoided meeting his eyes he cupped her face, forcing her to confront him.

'Do you really *know* what you're saying?' he demanded almost roughly. 'This isn't a game, and I'm not a boy, Miranda. Once——'

'I think you're probably right,' she interrupted him huskily. 'Maybe the only way to stop these dreams is——'

'Is that why you want me—to put an end to your dreams?'

He almost sounded angry, bitter. He had moved slightly away from her and her body, which had been so warm, so overheated, now felt chilled...abandoned...rejected almost. She ached to press closer to him, to close the unwanted gap between them, but she didn't have that kind of self-confidence, that degree of sureness about her own sensuality.

'Answer me,' he demanded brusquely.

She shook her head, honesty compelling her to admit the truth. 'No. No, it isn't. I want you. I want you because you make me ache so much that...'

She broke off, shaking her head, unable to go on, unable to articulate her feelings...her needs without embarrassment, unable to trust herself to admit how much she wanted him physically without admitting also how much she loved him.

As it was, she was afraid she had said too much...betrayed too much. It was all very well for a man to articulate his needs...his desires, but for a woman to do the same...

She needn't have been afraid. The hand cupping her face softened, his thumb stroking her skin gently as though reassuring her, his eyes dark with need and responsiveness to her as he told her, 'You make me ache as well.'

When he bent his head and kissed her, it was an almost passionless kiss, a gentle reassurance, a sealing of some unspoken pact almost, his mouth warm and reassuring, her own vulnerable, clinging softly to his as he released her and then turned her, his arm around her as he guided her towards the door, and then through it and up the stairs.

His bedroom door was open. She could see through it into the darkened room beyond, where only the moonlight showed the vague shadowy outline of his bed, large and old-fashioned with a headboard and footboard.

She stepped forward hesitantly, knowing that when she crossed the threshold into his room she crossed the threshold into a totally new world, a world of which she was still a little afraid, a world which was ultimately going to give her great pain.

But she had already made her decision and it was too late to change her mind now even if she had wanted to, which she did not. Her body yearned for him too much, ached for him too much, hungered for him too much for her to deny its needs now, no matter how much her mind might warn her against what she was doing.

However, as she made to step forward, Ben stopped her, his arm across the doorway barring her progress.

She gave him a startled, nervous look, wondering bleakly if he had changed his mind, if that perception of his had somehow or other warned him that what she felt for him wasn't merely a physical need. Instinct told her that he was the kind of man who would never knowingly allow a woman to believe he cared for her more than he did; that he would never use the word 'love' when he meant the word 'lust'; that, if he knew how she really felt about him he would not make love to her; but it seemed she was wrong and that her secret was safe, because he simply said a little roughly, 'Forgive me if this is old-fashioned of me and unnecessarily macho. It isn't intended to be; it's just that this is something I've been fantasising about doing ever since we...ever since I started dreaming about you.'

His slight hesitation, his pause before correcting himself and finishing what he was saying barely impinged upon her as she watched him and waited.

He removed the barrier of his arm and bent towards her, drawing her up against him, touching her mouth with his, lightly at first as though savouring a much longed-for delicacy, and then more deeply, more slowly, more compellingly, so that when he actually lifted her off her feet and into his arms she could only stare at him with be-mused eyes and her lips still moist, still trembling slightly from their contact with his.

When he actually carried her across to the bed, she could scarcely believe it. It was so opposed to everything she had ever gleaned about modern sexual manners, so unexpected, so...so...so tender and protective, so cherishing and caring.

That one simple gesture, so ridiculed and con-sidered unnecessary in modern-day sexuality, caught her so unawares, made her feel so...so soft...so female...so precious somehow, that she almost choked on the unfamiliar mixture of pain and sweetness that clogged her throat.

Here was a man, a modern man, who knew and accepted a woman's right to define her own life, to be independent, to have a right and a need to succeed and be judged as an equal in the outer male-orientated world of commerce, and yet who at the same time knew instinctively that there was a time when that same woman wanted all the cherishing, all the tenderness, all the caring that highlighted and underlined the superiority of his male strength and the vulnerability of her feminine weakness, without in any way exploiting them, without using them threateningly or punishingly.

And neither had there been anything theatrical about what he had done.

Logic and reality told her that in this day and age a woman made her own decision to have sex with a man; that she was perfectly capable of walking to his bed unaided and once there, equally capable of removing her own clothes; and yet as Ben held her close to him, smoothing the hair back off her face, kissing her skin, her closed eyelids, her cheekbone, her mouth, before gently removing her clothes, she admitted that there was a special sweetly erotic seduction in the act, a special feeling of tenderness, of being desired, that made her tremble a little in anticipation of the physical loving they would share, and her fear that because it was 'just sex', merely physical, it would somehow be degrading and leave an ashen, sour taste in her mouth vanished.

If he couldn't, didn't love her, then at least he had respect for her and for himself; at least she knew now that this would be no greedy, empty coming together, that they would share something that would be very special.

'Look at me.'

She opened her eyes in obedience to his command. He had slipped off his robe, and the moonlight showed her the satin width of his shoulders, the breadth and strength of his chest before it tapered to his waist, to the hard flatness of his belly and the thick dark arrowing of hair that marked it.

It showed her also the hard muscles of his thighs, the open extent of his arousal.

'It's still not too late,' he told her softly, 'if you want to change your mind...'

She shook her head quickly, and then shivered as her body reacted compulsively to the sight of his, her muscles tightening, her nipples peaking and hardening at the same time as her breasts seemed to swell and lift, warm and sweetly curved soft-fleshed fruits, designed by nature surely not just for the purpose of motherhood, but also to fit so sweetly into a man's hands, to invite by their very softness, their very round smooth-fleshedness the exploration of his mouth and the sharply passionate bite of his teeth.

She shivered again at what she was thinking, leaning yearningly towards him, wanting him now with an intensity, a completeness that made her feel more sure, more strong than she had ever felt in her whole life.

When he held her, kissed her, lifted her on to the bed, following her there, to hold her fast against him, she gave a small ecstatic sigh of delight.

*This* was what her body had been made for; this was why she had been given soft flesh and smooth curves, skin so silken that it invited the hungry glide of a man's hands, curves so tender that it made him shake just to know them.

She arched herself against him, a soft sound of happiness purring in her throat as she smoothed her hands down his back and licked exploratively at the satin hardness of his shoulder. The way he reacted, the way he tensed and told her roughly what she was doing to him, how she was making him feel, only incited her to go on stroking, kissing, licking, biting, until he groaned out loud and grabbed hold of her, kissing her throat, her shoulder, her arm and then her breast with such intensity that she went boneless and supine, her heart jerking almost painfully hard inside her while her body was filled with so much need, so much pleasure, so much sensation that she cried out to him that it was more than she could bear, that she wanted him, needed him, ached for him in so many ways that she was afraid she might die from the sheer glory of it.

She didn't, though. Instead she discovered that she could make *him* tremble and cry out; that her touch could make him moan and beg for surcease in a hoarse, strained voice that her nerve-endings quivered to hear.

When he entered her, she welcomed the controlled, almost gentle thrust of his body with such wild abandon and eagerness that she overrode his control, destroying it completely, so that when he tensed, hesitated, and told her in a low rough voice that he must withdraw from her, she wound herself even more tightly around him, refusing to let him leave her, seducing him with the soft rhythmic movements of her body until he groaned out loud in haunted anguish, knowing that the compellingly rhythmic movements of her body were defeating his will-power, taking from him almost the satisfaction he had felt it necessary to deny them both.

When he couldn't stand it any longer he moved within her so powerfully, so deeply that she cried out in shock at the intensity of her own pleasure, of her need to open her body so completely to him that he would penetrate its deepest, most sacred mysteries.

The fierce rigours of her climax were so unexpected, so unknown that she was completely unprepared for their almost violently physical effects, and for the draining weakness that engulfed her seconds later when she had felt the hot pulse of Ben's release inside her, her body thrilling in her feminine power to incite it, even if the weakness that followed left her shivering and trembling caught between tears and laughter, experiencing both fulfillment and exhaustion, content to lie breathless and damp in Ben's arms, while he smoothed her as he would have done a cat, his hand smoothing down over her back until the nervous trembling had left her body.

As she closed her eyes and felt herself drifting, floating on a delicious cloud into sleep, she whispered drowsily, 'It wasn't like my dreams at all. I never——'

'You never what?' Ben interrupted her.

She opened her eyes reluctantly; her head was resting on his shoulder and in the moonlight she could see a bead of sweat on his throat. She moved her head and absorbed it on to her tongue, gently savouring the hot male scent of him, enjoying the heat and taste of him before she closed her eyes again, moving luxuriously against him as she stretched her body next to his.

'You never what?' Ben repeated.

Too relaxed and happy to guard her words, she smiled. 'I never knew it could be like that,' she confessed softly.

Half asleep, later thinking that she must have imagined it, she heard him responding starkly, 'No, neither did I.'

Once more before morning they made love, slowly and sweetly so that Miranda was achingly aware of the gently inexorable tide of her own desire, of her need to savour and cherish each moment of their being together, each touch, each caress, and put a special yearning tenderness into each movement of her hands against his flesh, each drift of her lips welcoming the intimacy her caresses made him cry out for, loving the knowledge that he wanted her, ached for her.

This time her climax was less earth-shattering: rounder, sweeter somehow, leaving her bathed in satisfaction and joy. In the dim light she saw that there were marks on his skin, inflicted by her nails and teeth when she had had to stifle the words of love she ached to give him.

Love-bites. She smiled sadly to herself. These were certainly that, given in place of the words, the vows, the love she knew she could not burden him with.

Whatever else happened she would never regret that she had had this time with him, she vowed as he drew her sleepily towards him, holding her, cradling her, surrounding her still with tenderness and care.

Only when she was sure he was properly asleep did she ease herself away from him, padding silently towards the door, clutching her clothes.

Downstairs and dressed, she took a small notepad from her bag and penned him a brief note.

It read simply, 'Thank you for last night. Let's hope that from now on we both have dreamless sleep, but it isn't an experiment I feel it would be wise to repeat.'

As she folded it and left it prominently displayed on the table, she knew he would understand what she was saying. That she had no regrets about what they had done, but that it was something that wasn't going to be repeated, not because she didn't want to. Her mouth twisted wryly.

There were going to be many, many nights, years from now, when she would lie sleepless and aching, reliving this night, and wishing with all her might that he were there beside her; but it wasn't just sex she wanted from him. She wanted it all: commitment, caring...permanence, children...and most of all she wanted his love.

She respected him for not tainting what they had with false words of love, with meaningless promises. He had praised her body, her responsiveness, her ability to arouse and delight him, lavishing the soft words on her, heaping her with the gift of his pleasure in all that they were sharing, allowing her the freedom, giving her the self-confidence to give her sensuality a free rein without holding anything back from him—anything, that was, other than those betraying words of love.

It was just growing light when she got into her car and drove away. She prayed that when he read her note he would respect her enough not to try to change her mind, not to diminish what they had shared.

It proved even harder than she had envisaged.

When she got home she went upstairs to shower, pausing as she stood there, reluctant to wash the scent of him from her skin, her stomach muscles quivering with remembered pleasure as she saw the small bruise marks forming on her body. Her breasts swelled tormentingly, aching...

Angrily she stepped under the shower and turned on the cold water, gasping with shock as she stood beneath the icy spray.

She had been at work for an hour when Liz arrived.

'Good heavens!' she exclaimed as she walked in and saw her. 'You're an early bird.'

'I've got quite a lot of paperwork to catch up on with Dad being away,' Miranda responded, turning her back on her as she added with studied control, 'Oh, and, by the way, should Ben Frobisher ring and ask for me, would you tell him that I'm either out or engaged?'

There was a small silence and then Liz replied gently, 'If you're sure that's what you want.'

Her gentleness was almost too much for Miranda to bear. She tensed her body against her own vulnerability, and said in a hard voice, 'Yes, that's what I want.'

Liz didn't say anything more, but Miranda could guess what she must be thinking. She too had been a guest at the wedding, and must have seen that Miranda and Ben had been paired off together... must have drawn her own conclusions from that, just as she was doing now from the instructions Miranda had given her. No doubt she would assume they had had a quarrel...a row...but she was discreet and kind and she would keep her thoughts to herself, which was just as well. In the run-up to the wedding, Miranda had received more than one sly comment about it being time she herself settled down, accompanied by unsubtle references to Ben. Well, the gossip would soon die down without anything to fuel it.

Halfway through the morning, Liz slipped out to buy some sandwiches. When she came back she was practically running, unable to hide her shock as she burst into the office.

'Miranda, there's been an accident!' she announced breathlessly. 'I heard about it in the sandwich shop. It's Ben Frobisher.'

Ben. Miranda froze, getting out of her chair before saying, 'Ben? What . . . ?'

'I'm not sure. Something about problems with the building contracter. No one seems to know exactly what happened . . . only that there was an accident . . . something about an internal wall collapsing. Miranda . . . where are you going?' she protested as Miranda raced towards the door. 'It's no use going there,' she called worriedly after her as Miranda flung the door open and ran across the square in the direction of the High Street, ignoring the surprised stares of the people who stopped to watch her.

Shaking her head, Liz finished her sentence. 'It's no use going there. They've already taken him to hospital. At least, that's what they said in the sandwich shop.'

There was a small cluster of people outside the house in the High Street, the same cluster that gathered to watch men digging a hole in the road, or the scene of an accident. Impatiently Miranda pushed her way through them, ignoring the protest of a burly man who had been talking to one of the onlookers, darting in through the open door as he called out after her, 'Hey, you can't go in there.'

A shaft of sunlight illuminated the bare interior of the hallway; she noticed absently that it came from an upper storey and recognised that Ben must have gone ahead with the renovators' suggestion for redesigning the stairwell. The sunlight was thick with dust, arid and choking; it clung to her skin, powdering it, the air tasting old and dank when she breathed in.

As she looked upwards she could see a pile of rubble—bricks, plaster, pieces of wood—and her heart jerked fearfully inside her chest. She held her breath, trying to stifle her fear, her pain, slowly making her way up the temporary wooden staircase until she was on a level with the collapsed wall. What she had seen from below had simply been a small part of the devastation. Now that she was on a level with it she could see the magnitude of what was happening.

An entire interior wall appeared to have collapsed, spewing bricks and plaster everywhere. She could see through the gap in the wall quite clearly into the room beyond it.

Trembling now, she walked towards it. The house was empty, quiet; there was just her and the dust her coming had disturbed to swirl heavily around her.

As she reached the fallen masonry she saw something lying on the floor. A jacket . . . Ben's jacket, surely.

Trembling, she bent down and picked it up, pressing the soft fabric to her cheek. Yes, it was his. It smelled of him. Her fingers closed on it compulsively. Where was he? How badly was he hurt? If only she had known... been here... She felt the pain, the panic, building up inside her, a huge tearing agony she couldn't contain.

Tears pricked her eyes, and as she blinked them away she saw the blood on the jacket.

A long agonised moan of pain ripped her throat, she dropped to her knees, pressing the jacket to her face, protesting on a tortured moan.

'No... please... Ben... Ben!'

'Miranda.'

The shock of hearing him say her name spun her round, her eyes huge with disbelief as her tears rolled down her dusty face.

'What is it? What are you doing here? This floor isn't safe.'

He was coming towards her, reaching her as she stood up, repeating almost angrily, 'What are you doing here? Why are you here?'

'I heard... I thought you'd been hurt.'

She saw suddenly that he had been, that his shirt sleeve was rolled back and that there was blood on his arm. She swayed as she saw it, shivering when he reached out to steady her.

'It's only a cut,' he told her roughly, stopping when he saw that she was clutching his jacket. 'So, you thought I'd been hurt. And that's why you came rushing round here. Am I supposed to believe *that* after the note I found this morning?'

He was angry, she recognised, flinching back from him.

'Or were you hoping that I *had* been injured...that a few tons of falling bricks might have conveniently deprived me of all memory of last night?' He gave her a savage, wolfish smile. 'Well, let me tell you this: the whole damned building could have fallen on me before that could happen.'

She couldn't bear the pain of what he was saying to her, and reacted to it instinctively, denying his words, crying out to him, 'No, you're wrong! I didn't——'

'You didn't what, Miranda? You didn't walk out on me, leaving me a polite little note saying thanks but no thanks? Well, that wasn't the message I received.'

He was angry, and not just angry, but bitter as well.

'No, please...it wasn't like that. You don't understand.'

'Then explain it to me. Tell me why, after the most perfect loving I can ever remember, I woke up this morning to find you gone and that chilly polite little note waiting for me.'

She shook her head despairingly. 'I can't...I can't explain.'

'You mean you *won't*.'

She started to shiver. 'You're angry with me.'

'Angry with you?' He gave her a biting, incredulous look, pushing his fingers through his hair, his body tense and aggressive. 'My God, you're speaking like a child. You *must* have known.'

A shout from below interrupted them. Miranda watched as Ben went to the head of the stairs and called back, 'Yes, I'm up here. Any news from the hospital?'

'Yes,' the other man called back. 'He's going to be OK. Lucky bastard. After what he tried to do, he doesn't deserve it.'

'And his wife's been informed?' Ben wanted to know.

'Yes, we did as you instructed and made sure someone took her out to the hospital. Oh, and Jack Meade said to tell you he'll have the men in after lunch to make everything safe.'

'Thanks, Rob.'

Miranda watched as Rob, the man who had been guarding the front door, went back to his post, leaving the two of them alone.

Her throat felt stiff and sore, and, now that the initial shock of believing that Ben had been hurt and then discovering that he was safe was over, she felt oddly weak, as fragile as though her body could hardly support the burden of her emotions.

'What happened?'

The words sounded disembodied, vague and uncertain.

She watched as Ben turned round and studied her.

'We're not totally sure as yet, but it seems that Charlesworth decided to have another go at making his dislike of me felt, only this time he misjudged things badly, and the wall he had been tampering with, no doubt hoping to cause a set-back and more expense for me, collapsed on top of him.

'Luckily I was here at the time. I had just come in, heard the commotion and got up here just in time to drag him free. He'd been stunned by a falling brick when the wall first started to collapse. He was damned lucky he wasn't killed.'

Miranda closed her eyes. She was trembling all over, visibly shaking as she recognised what Ben wasn't telling—that he, in saving Ralph, had been equally at risk.

'Miranda.' His voice sharpened with anxiety, as he came towards her, demanding roughly, 'What is it? What's wrong?'

He had reached her, was touching her before she could evade him, the sensation of his fingers on her arm, even with the thickness of her shirt between them, making her feel so vulnerable that she tensed immediately and tried to pull back, her face empty of all colour, its pallor heightened by its coating of dust.

'You've been crying.'

The husky comment made her focus on him, her eyes dark and frantic.

'I told you; I thought you'd been hurt,' she repeated dully.

She was still holding his jacket and, as though she suddenly realised how betraying her behaviour was, she opened her fingers and dropped it.

Ben stared down at her for a few seconds and then bent to pick it up.

She started to tremble again, even more violently than before.

'Miranda.' His voice was heavy and sombre and a knife-like pain sliced through her. He had guessed the truth she was trying to conceal. He was going to confront her with it; she couldn't endure that... couldn't endure his compassion, his pity...

'No.' She tore herself free of him, almost flinging herself down the stairs and darting out of the building, much to the surprise of the small crowd still gathered there.

When she got back to the office, Liz was waiting for her, her face creased with concern.

'Miranda.'

'I don't want to talk about it,' she told her tightly.

She walked into her own office and closed the door, walking unsteadily over to her desk and sitting down in her chair. She was shaking again, even more than before. She was crying as well, she realised, as she felt the wetness on her skin and the shudders that tore at her chest and hurt her throat.

Putting her head down on her desk she gave in to her emotions and wept.

When she heard her office door open, she didn't bother to lift her head. Her tears had exhausted her. Drained her. She had no energy, no will, no ability to do anything.

'It's no good, Liz,' she said in a low, exhausted voice. 'I can't help it, I love Ben Frobisher and it's never ever going to get any better... never ever going to go away.'

'I'm very glad to hear it.'

'Ben!'

She lifted her head, her lips framing his name, but no sound emerged as shock held her in its grip.

In disbelief she watched as he closed her office door and came towards her, half dragging her out of her chair and holding her against him as he demanded roughly, 'Tell me that again.'

Tell him what?

He must have recognised her confusion, because he said, half impatiently, like a man trying desperately to exercise restraint, 'Tell me that you love me, dammit!'

When she flinched, unable to endure his cruel mockery of her, trying to break free of him, he shifted his weight so that she was trapped between his body and her desk, and then cupped her face, forcing her to look back at him.

'Miranda, what is it?' he demanded rawly. 'What the hell have I done to make you act like this? When I ask you to tell me that you love me, you flinch away from me as though I'm threatening to torture you.'

'Aren't you?' she demanded achingly, shuddering as her body registered the heat and intimacy of his.

'That wasn't my intention, no,' he told her drily. 'I recognise that an independent career-minded woman might not relish the knowledge that a man loves her and wants her love in return, but I hadn't realised it would cause her so much revulsion that it would make her physically cringe away from him. I'm only human, Miranda,' he told her rawly. 'I can't help it. If my love for you makes me want to elicit the same response from you, makes me ache to hear you say that you love me, and I can't help feeling bitter...cheated almost that your need to remain independent means that you'd rather deny what you feel.'

He felt her tension and gave her a tired look.

'What did you think I was going to do—use the fact that you loved me to force you into some kind of permanent commitment.' He shook his head. 'I can't deny that's what I *want* from you, but only if it's given freely. I'm not going to pretend I don't want you as my wife, that I don't want to share the rest of my life with you, but I love you too much to force that kind of situation on you. Don't you understand? I love you enough to accept that you want your freedom.'

Tears were sliding down her face. He trapped one with his thumb, stroking her skin, watching her with loving, concerned eyes.

'You don't understand,' she managed to tell him. 'I didn't *know* you loved me. I thought it was just...just sex.'

His mouth twisted as he looked at her.

'Just sex...my love...just sex *is* never, *could* never come anywhere near being like what we shared.'

'But you didn't say anything. Didn't tell me.'

'I may not have given you the words, but my love for you was in every touch, every kiss. I thought you must surely know that. I thought that was why you left me...why you wrote me that callous, chilly little note, because you were rejecting that love.'

She shook her head.

'No. I just didn't want to burden you with mine.' She shivered and asked him anxiously, 'Do you really love me? I'm not sure any of this is actually real.'

'It's real,' he assured her softly, 'and what's even more real is the fact that just as soon as your father and Helen get back, you and I are going to be married.' He paused and looked at her, hesitating for a second before asking her uncertainly, 'You *do* want to marry me, don't you?'

This time it was joy that made her tremble as she wound her arms around his neck and whispered tremulously, 'Yes. Yes, I do.'

'Mm. Alone at last,' Ben teased, as Miranda sat down on the bed of their honeymoon hotel, easing off her shoes.

It had been a long flight from Heathrow to this remote tropical island and the privacy of their own private bungalow in the spectacular grounds of the island's single hotel.

'Yes. I couldn't believe it when Susan Charlesworth turned up at the wedding on her own, could you? She's going to divorce Ralph, so she told Helen. Helen even suspects that she might have found someone else. Well, good luck to her if she has. I must admit, I never thought she'd find the will-power to leave him.'

'I don't want to talk about Ralph Charlesworth or anyone else,' Ben told her positively, taking hold of her, and adding softly, 'In fact, I don't want to talk about anything at all. Mm ... you taste good,' he added thickly as his lips teased her throat.

Miranda felt her body begin to soften and ache.

'I'm all hot and sticky,' she protested. 'I was going to have a shower.'

'Good idea,' Ben agreed, smiling at her with a look in his eyes that made her muscles tighten and her heartbeat quicken.

'It frightens me sometimes how easily we might not have met,' she told him breathlessly as he drew her to her feet, and reached behind her for the zip of her dress. 'If I hadn't bumped into you by accident. If we had simply walked past one another...' She snuggled up to him blissfully.

She felt the small explosion that shook his body and looked at him suspiciously.

'What are you laughing at?' she demanded.

'You didn't bump into me "by accident", my love.'

She withdrew slightly from him, giving him a narrow-eyed accusatory look.

'If you think that I deliberately——' she began indignantly, but he stopped, placing his finger against her lips, his eyes full of laughter as he shook his head.

'No ... not you.' When she stared at him, he told her wryly, 'I'd already walked round that corner and seen you coming towards me, head down, hurrying, oblivious to my existence, while I ... while

I,' he continued softly, 'had taken one look at you, and known... known immediately that you were the one, my other half.' He shrugged as she stared at him in silence.

'Oh, I know it sounds theatrical... dramatic. It shook me, I can tell you. Half of me couldn't really believe it, didn't really want to believe it... but the other half... the other half had turned me round, walked me back round that corner, made me wait and then...'

'And then I walked into you,' Miranda said slowly. 'And all this time I've thought... I felt...' She swallowed. 'I thought it was just me,' she told him huskily. 'That I must be going crazy, to take one look at a man, and to feel about him as I'd never, ever felt about anyone in my whole life... to think about him so obsessively that within hours of meeting him I was imagining... wanting... And then those dreams...'

'Yes, I know,' he told her sombrely. 'It was hard for both of us. You were so antagonistic towards me that I could not, dared not, let you see you affected me.'

'I wasn't antagonistic towards you when you kissed me to save me from Ralph,' she pointed out slyly.

'No, not then, and I clung to that small seed of hope, willing it to take root, to grow... and at the same time everywhere I went I kept on hearing about how determined you were to remain single, how important your career was to you. How everyone who knew you had heard your views on marriage and motherhood. How you'd avoided both as though they were dangerous as lime pits.'

'I'd already recognised that my views were starting to change before I met you,' she confessed, leaning her head against his shoulder. 'Each time I held a baby...played with a child, something ached inside me, although it took me a long time to admit to myself that that ache was caused by a need I'd refused to acknowledge I could feel, never mind fulfil. How could I have a child when I didn't have a husband...didn't have a lover? And then I met you.'

'Ah-ha! I see, so it wasn't really me you wanted, just my——'

She silenced him, shaking her head at him as he laughed at her.

'It most certainly *was* you,' she corrected him. 'I took one look at you, and all those feelings, all those needs I'd heard so much about but never experienced were suddenly there.'

'Are they still there?' he asked her teasingly.

'We can discuss that after I've had my shower.'

'Mm. I've got a better idea. Why don't we discuss it while *we're* having *our* shower?'

Later, fulfilled and drowsy, curled up next to him, when he touched her mouth with his fingertip and asked her what she was thinking, she turned towards him and said seriously, 'I was just wondering about our bathroom at the house.'

He had purchased the house from the trustees of the estate the week before they were married, although it was going to be many months before they could move into it. In the meantime they were going to live in her cottage.

'What about it?'

'I'm glad we decided to include a shower as well as a bath,' she told him sleepily, cuddling up to him while he laughed and kissed her and told her he loved her.

'I love you too,' she whispered sleepily into his skin. 'I love you too.'

# Accept 4 Free Romances and 2 Free gifts

**• F R O M   R E A D E R   S E R V I C E •**

An irresistible invitation from Mills & Boon Reader Service. Please accept our offer of 4 free Romances, a CUDDLY TEDDY and a special MYSTERY GIFT... Then, if you choose, go on to enjoy 6 captivating Romances every month for just £1.60 each, postage and packing free. Plus our FREE newsletter with author news, competitions and much more.

**Send the coupon below to:**
**Reader Service, FREEPOST, PO Box 236, Croydon, Surrey CR9 9EL.**

✂- - - - - - - - - - - - ▐ NO STAMP REQUIRED ▌- - - - - - - - - - -

**Yes!** Please rush me my 4 free Romances and 2 free gifts! Please also reserve me a Reader Service Subscription. If I decide to subscribe I can look forward to receiving 6 new Romances each month for just £9.60, postage and packing is free. If I choose not to subscribe I shall write to you within 10 days - I can keep the books and gifts whatever I decide. I may cancel or suspend my subscription at any time. I am over 18 of age.

Name Mrs/Miss/Ms/Mr _____    EP17R

Address _____

_____

Postcode _____ Signature _____

Offer expires 31st May 1992. The right is reserved to refuse an application and change the terms of this offer. Readers overseas and in Eire please send for details. Southern Africa write to Independant Book Services, Postbag X3010, Randburg 2125. You may be mailed with offers from other reputable companies as a result of this application.

If you would prefer not to share in this opportunity, please tick box ☐

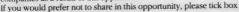

# Next month's Romances

Each month, you can choose from a world of variety in romance with Mills & Boon. These are the new titles to look out for next month.

**NO GENTLE SEDUCTION** Helen Bianchin

**THE FINAL TOUCH** Betty Neels

**TWIN TORMENT** Sally Wentworth

**JUNGLE ENCHANTMENT** Patricia Wilson

**DANCE FOR A STRANGER** Susanne McCarthy

**THE DARK SIDE OF DESIRE** Michelle Reid

**WITH STRINGS ATTACHED** Vanessa Grant

**BARRIER TO LOVE** Rosemary Hammond

**FAR FROM OVER** Valerie Parv

**HIJACKED HONEYMOON** Eleanor Rees

**DREAMS ARE FOR LIVING** Natalie Fox

**PLAYING BY THE RULES** Kathryn Ross

**ONCE A CHEAT** Jane Donnelly

**HEART IN FLAMES** Sally Cook

**KINGFISHER MORNING** Charlotte Lamb

*STARSIGN*

**STING IN THE TAIL** Annabel Murray

Available from Boots, Martins, John Menzies, W.H. Smith, Woolworths and other paperback stockists.

Also available from Mills and Boon Reader Service, P.O. Box 236, Thornton Road, Croydon, Surrey CR9 3RU.